White Water

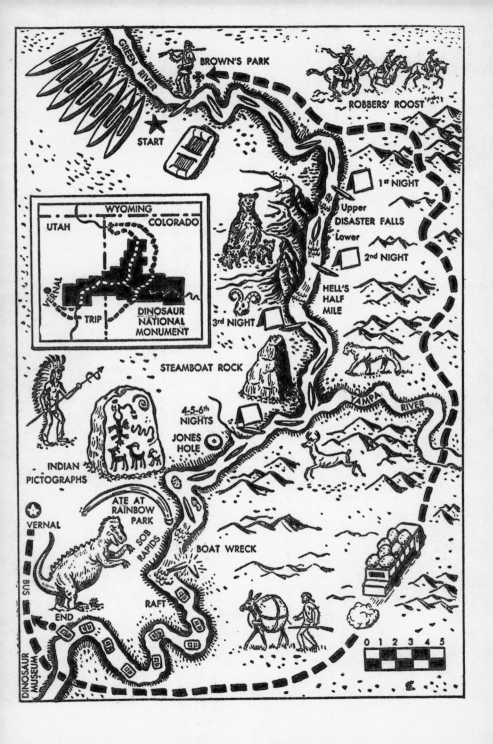

White Water

by
VIVIAN BRECK

Doubleday & Company, Inc.
Garden City, New York

For B. A. T.

The spark behind this book

White Water

CHAPTER ONE

The living room of the Dawson house on San Francisco's Russian Hill looked as if a hurricane had just come swirling through it. Nothing was where it belonged. Nothing, that is, except the grand piano which the hurricane had not been strong enough to move out of the way. Chairs, tables, lamps, books, and magazines, even the big davenport, had been pushed aside, huddled up against the walls of the room to clear the center of the floor.

The name of the hurricane was not Betsy or Connie or Diane. Nor had it originated in the conflicting air currents of the Caribbean. The name of this particular storm was Andrea Dawson. And at the moment all that could be seen of her was a pair of bare legs and two bare feet waving in the air. The rest of the girl was wedged inside a fourteen foot foldboat which writhed and wriggled on the rug as if it were filled with a whole family of jumping kangaroos.

All around the boat, in fact all around the room, were scattered the bits and pieces which would finally be assembled into one unit ready for launching. There were float balls and paddles, a spray deck, seat cushion, back rest, and what looked like enough ribs and

stringers to stiffen half a dozen canvas boats. The long
thin carrying bag and the short square carrying bag
were draped over the back of an overstuffed chair which
blocked off the fireplace. A couple of blown-up inner
tubes destined to be pushed into the bow and stern
were lying near the hall doorway ready to trip any vis-
itor to the living room. And over the neck of a brass
reading lamp hung a bright orange Mae West which
looked massive enough to hold not only Andrea Dawson's head and shoulders but her whole body out of the
water.

From under the forward deck, where the main wrig-
gling was going on, came muffled sounds which an opti-
mist might have interpreted as singing. Then abruptly
the concert stopped as Andy extricated herself. With
a sigh she stood up to stretch cramped muscles.

"It isn't right," she muttered. "It just isn't right and
it's got to be right. For Lodore—one hundred per cent
right. I've got to be an expert."

Lodore! Every time she said the word a little shiver
went down her spine—a delicious shiver—of excitement
and bravado and a little scariness all omeleted together.
The canyon of Lodore. The very name oozed mystery.
Haunt of the golden eagle and wild Canadian goose,
canyon the Indians feared because they believed malig-
nant spirits haunted the cliffs, waiting to snatch away
any traveler who dared the sacred waters.

To take a foldboat down the rapids of Lodore was
something. It really was. Something! But Chuck had
said she was good enough. She was not a beginner any
more and Chuck, the old past master of foldboating,
the champion of all the River Runners, had said she
could go.

The song she had been chanting inside the boat, if
anything so tuneless could be called a song, came back
to her lips. Actually the words were part of an old poem.

The melody was her own invention. But lack of a tune never kept Andrea Dawson from singing—if she was alone. When other people were around she kept her wide red mouth carefully closed. Being laughed at was a thing Andy could not endure. Alone, singing was her safety valve, her way of letting some of the excitement seething inside of her escape before she exploded into little pieces like a balloon. She began again.

"And grumbling and rumbling and tumbling,
And clattering and battering and shattering——"

Her voice swept up in a mighty shout.

"All at once and all o'er, with a mighty uproar,
And this way the water comes down
at Lo-do-O-O-ORE."

Here she put in a few fine operatic trills so that the whole room quivered with mock coloratura.

Just reading the names on the map of Lodore Canyon (and Andrea had poured over them for weeks) was enough to send chills down your backbone. "Flaming Gorge, Whirlpool Canyon, Disaster Falls, Hell's Half Mile." John Wesley Powell had named those rapids way back in 1869 when he first tried to get his clumsy wooden boats down the Green River to the Colorado. And all these years the names had stuck. With good reason, no doubt. But Chuck had already done it once and now he said she could do it. After only two years and a few months of foldboating he had okayed her to go with the River Runners. Well, she couldn't disappoint Chuck by asking for help before her boat even got into the water. She would put it together and take it apart until she knew the feel of every rib in the dark, the way she knew the furniture in her bedroom.

Andy had often helped set up a double foldboat. But for this trip Dad had at last given her a boat of her own,

a single, the exact thing she wanted. She smiled down
at the blue canvas deck, rubbed it with her hand as if
it might vanish away. Then, all business again, she began to search through the jumble of stuff on the floor
for the sheet of yellow paper on which directions for
setting up the foldboat were printed.

Instructions were set down in German, French, and
English. That in itself was exciting. Made you feel you
were part of a big international fraternity. The Europeans, of course, had been foldboating on their rivers
for years before Americans woke up to the fact that
they were missing a heavenly sport.

Paper in hand, Andy moved over to the big window
overlooking San Francisco Bay where the light was better. Only a European manufacturer would have been
so thrifty with paper. You almost needed a magnifying
glass to read the fine print. She looked again at the dia-
gram where all thirty-six parts were labeled with lines
and numbers. No help there. She went on to figure one,
slowly reading the words aloud. Figure two: "The two
floor sections are then hooked together in the center.
By effortlessly pressing down at this point, the boat
is stretched in the longitudinal direction."

Effortlessly indeed! She had pushed down till she
was blue in the face, till she was afraid of breaking the
floor ladder into splinters.

Andy's jaw set squarely as she went on reading. Then
with a burst of glee she shouted, "Howling hyenas!
What a dimwit!" Tossing the paper into the air, she
went at the boat again, yanking out the wooden ladder
lying along the bottom. Her mistake was ABC simple.
She had transposed the fore and aft sections of the
floor. They looked alike, but were different enough so
that the tough rubber hull refused to stretch over the
wrong one.

Once more her head went down and her voice soared rapturously.

"Advancing and prancing and glancing and dancing,
And curling and whirling and purling and twirling,
All at once and all o'er, with a mighty upROAR——"

It may not have been high C that Andy hit, but it was high something, when the sound of her sister's voice brought her tumbling back to earth.

"Andy! For crying out loud! *Must* you do this in the middle of the living-room floor?"

The answer to this question was lost in the innards of the foldboat.

"How can I possibly practice in here with you turning the place into a garage?" Marianne's voice was not angry. Just pained and exasperatingly gentle.

Andy knew exactly how Marianne was looking. The gray eyes in her delicate oval face would be hurt, even a touch disgusted, at the impropriety of the scene. A boat in the living room. How barbaric! But she couldn't stop now. Not when she had just figured out what was wrong and almost—almost—fixed it.

The ladder snapped into place at last—effortlessly. The hull became rigid and Andy backed out till she was kneeling on the rug. "But I haven't touched your piano," she cried. "*Or* your piano bench."

"Well, it's the only thing in the place you haven't moved," Marianne wailed. "It's—it's upsetting to practice in such confusion. Why couldn't you put your crackpot boat together somewhere else?"

Andrea mopped perspiration from her forehead onto the back of her hand, wiped the hand on her shorts. "Where?" she demanded. "In our bedroom maybe? On top of the twin beds? You'd love that."

"Oh, Andy, you're hopeless. Of course I don't mean

that. I mean out of doors somewhere, naturally. Where
a boat belongs."

"A boat belongs in the water."

"What's wrong with the sidewalk in front of our
house?"

"On this hill? All the parts would skid off into space.
If they didn't blow away first. Besides"—Andy made a
grab for the yellow sheet of instructions—"the directions
say, 'Assemble the boat on a *grassy* surface. Not on sand
or rock.'"

Marianne laughed. "I'm sure this ferocious canyon
you're heading for will be filled with well-clipped
lawns."

Andy grinned back at her sister, a broad radiant
grin. She was far too happy to let herself feel teased.
"Well, if you must know, the rug is nice and squishy
to kneel on. And the sidewalk isn't."

"How our parents ever managed to bring you up in
the middle of a city will forever remain a mystery,"
Marianne said. Picking her way gingerly among unfamiliar objects, she dropped a kiss on the top of Andy's
yellow head and sat down at the piano.

"What was that fancy aria I heard as I came in?"
Marianne's face was solemn, but a twinkle lurked at
the corners of her eyes.

"I won't sing any more. Scout's honor. At least not
while you're within earshot. I know it sears your soul.
But it isn't my fault I can't carry a tune. All the musical
genius in the family got used up on you." Andrea sighed
wistfully. "I still like to sing—when I'm happy."

Marianne let her hands drift idly over the keys, limber-
ing up her fingers before she began practicing in earnest.
"Come on, Andy. Give. I heard definite, if unfamiliar,
words coming out of that kayak. Have you taken up
composing poetry?"

"It isn't a kayak. It's a foldboat." Andy's tone was

passionate. "If it were a kayak I wouldn't have to assemble and knock it down every time——"

"All right, darling. It's a foldboat. But what on earth
were you bellowing with your head stuck in the cock-
pit? Or whatever that part of its anatomy is called."

"Oh, nothing." Andy shrugged. "Just some lines out
of a long rigamarole by Robert Southey. Actually it's
something he wrote for his children, but it's called *The
Cataract of Lodore*. I ran into the reference when I
looked up Lodore in the encyclopedia and thought it
would be fun to memorize some of it."

"And you'll sing it," Marianne said, sliding her fingers into the familiar melody, "In the evening, by the
moonlight . . ."

"Hush up and get on with your own busy work. Do
you think I dote on hearing you twiddle up and down
the keys over and over again in that Mozart thing you're
learning?"

Marianne laughed amiably, opened the music on the
rack, and, leaning forward a little, went at her practicing with dedicated concentration.

For a long moment Andy sat back on her heels on
the floor watching her sister's hands. What a funny
family we are, she thought. All so different—all five of
us. The only thing about us that's alike is that each
person is completely nuts about *something*. All except
Mother. Maybe she'd be that way, too, if she hadn't
had to divide herself up like a pie, giving each of us a
little slice of herself. Maybe she'd be a famous actress
by now if she hadn't been a doctor's wife with three
kids. Or maybe Mother's the nuttiest one of all—about
us.

Her eye drifted away from Marianne's supple, tapered hands, the scarlet tips flying up and down the
keyboard, and rested on her own. Brown square hands
they were, the nails clipped short as a boy's. It would

be nice to have Marianne's hands. Or Marianne's pretty face and small-boned body which fitted so neatly into size-ten clothes. Andy fought back the emotion which always rose in her when she thought seriously about her sister. Rebellion, envy? What was it?

As she mused on the Dawson family, her thoughts raced along. What a lot of pleasure Marianne gives with her music. And Dad—why a doctor spends his life helping other people. Then a smile skimmed her face as she considered the peculiarities of her twelve-year-old brother. Cute old Skeeter. With that brain of his Skeeter's bound to do something fabulous. But what have I ever done? Given my family a lot of worry and trouble and expense, that's all. And I suppose this trip to Lodore is going to give them more worry.

Well—moping won't put my boat together. Pushing dissatisfaction with herself down to the bottom of her mind, Andrea fitted the last two wooden ribs into her boat until it sat trim and taut on the thick brown rug. Float balls dangled fore and aft and even the tiny burgee intended to mark the wind flared jauntily from the bow.

When Dr. Erick Dawson came home late that afternoon he found his younger daughter sitting on the bottom of her new treasure with knees and toes braced against the wooden ribs of the foldboat. An orange life preserver was wrapped around her body and the double-bladed paddle sliced the air in time to Marianne's music.

"Hello!" he said. "Are we on the Blue Danube or down among the Volga boatmen?" Dragging back into place the biggest of the chairs which Andy had pushed askew, he settled into it, stretched out his long legs, and began to loosen the collar and tie which confined both his neck and his spirit.

"You're on the Green River—in Colorado," Andy

whispered melodramatically, "drifting with the current and watching the sunset on the fabulous cliffs of Lodore."

Tenderly she laid the paddle across the bow of the boat and beamed at her father. It was always nice having him get home. When those wide shoulders under the tweed jacket came through the front door a new feeling seemed to fill the house. A sort of nothing-bad-can-happen-now feeling. Once a guest at a dinner party the family were having had referred to Dad as tremendously dynamic, whatever that meant exactly. Maybe it was what her grandmother used to call "full of get-up-and-git." Skeeter no doubt would have the definition cold, because a dynamo had something to do with electricity.

Marianne struck the closing chords of Mozart and swung around on the piano bench to speak to her father.

"Play some Chopin for me, Babe," he begged.

"M-maybe. What time is it? I'm cook tonight. Mother's down the peninsula somewhere with the 'girls'—swimming. Said she didn't intend to get back till dinner was *all* ready."

The big man in the big chair looked at his wrist watch. "Five-forty—more or less. How about you, Andy? Could you come ashore long enough to get dinner started?"

Again Andrea thought, Making music gives other people pleasure. Foldboats give them—— "I'll do it," she said, starting to unfasten the life preserver. "Especially if you will push some of the furniture back into place for me. What are we having?"

Marianne announced the menu. "Baked fish, tossed lettuce, baked potatoes."

"Sounds simple."

"Mother left the fish all ready to pop into the oven.

And don't forget to oil the potato skins before you put
them in."

Andy turned in the doorway to give her sister a look
intended to convey the idea that she had been turning
out peerless baked potatoes for years and years.

"Also there's a gigantic bag of peas to shell. I'll be
along to help as soon as old man Chopin gets Dad un-
wound."

Feeling drenched in nobility, Andy went off to take
Marianne's turn in the kitchen.

Dr. Erick Dawson believed in learning by doing.
"Most city-bred youngsters," he often said, "don't have
enough essential chores. They're cheated out of responsibility." Acting on this conviction, both he and his
wife insisted that not only their daughters, but their
son also, should be made ready to cope with a do-it-
yourself world by sharing the household routines until
they could whip through them nonchalantly and effi-
ciently.

"If one of my girls marries a farmer," Dr. Dawson
had been heard to remark, "she may have to be introduced to the cows, but the stove and vacuum cleaner
will be old friends."

So far as it was possible the young Dawsons were
also urged to do their own thinking. They went to pub-
lic schools with other children in their neighborhood,
but when it came time for college each child made his
own choice.

Two years ago, because of its outstanding music department, Marianne had decided on a small co-educa-
tional college in southern California. Also, Marianne
liked dates.

Skeeter—well, Skeeter managed to shatter all his parents' theories of education. He had such a detailed
mechanical knowledge of automobiles, such a passion

for every rivet, bolt, and fender of a car, that it was hard to get him to pay attention to anything else. Before arriving in the first grade he had taught himself to read. Billboards were his primer. His storybooks were the advertising folders put out by automobile companies. As a result the first grade bored him into a rage. When spelling came into his life he flatly refused to bother with it.

"I'll have a seccatary when I'm grown up," he told the teacher who begged him to write "which" instead of "wich." "Seccataries can spell."

The next day he was discovered idly covering pages with words like carburetor, crankshaft, and differential, all spelled quite correctly.

Regretfully his parents sent him off at last to a boarding school which specialized in college preparatory work. After a month he wrote home.

"Dear Dad: You are wasting your money keeping me in this place, for you would not approve of this place at all. It is awfully authorytarian and you have always taught us we ought to think for ourselfs. Gosh, if they could around here, they would also tell you how to breethe."

Skeeter's boarding-school career ended after one term and he came home to pursue his own way of life and learning. This consisted of daydreaming until 3 P.M. on Monday, Tuesday, Wednesday, Thursday, and Friday. The rest of the time he lived—watching automobiles, reading about automobiles, or haunting the garage where they were being repaired.

Andy's education had turned out to be different both from Marianne's and from Skeeter's. Four years ago, when she was thirteen, it had been tragically interrupted. The interruption altered not only her whole way of life but her character.

Marianne let the melting notes of the nocturne die away before she spoke. "Enough, Dad?"

"Never enough," he said fondly. "But I suppose you'd better take over on dinner so Andy can put her boat away before Mother comes home to this ungodly mess."

Marianne shook her head despairingly. "The child is mad. But mad! I'd be willing to bet she goes through this routine tomorrow and *every* day until she leaves town."

"And you'll practice the piano every day, won't you?" her father asked, rubbing one thumb against the bowl of a warm pipe.

"Touché," Marianne said, smiling. "But seriously, Dad, aren't you a little bothered about Andy's going off on this trip? Sounds awfully rugged—for her."

"It *will* be rugged. But I think it's a chance we have to take. Something she has to do—alone. Andy has walled herself off from certain parts of life and I hope, *we* hope . . ." He let the sentence trail unfinished. "Anyhow, I'm not really worried. I had a private talk with Chuck Tormey. He feels Andy is fully equal to taking her boat through the Lodore rapids. Promised to hold her down if she gets any of her rash notions. Still 'n' all, I'll be glad when she's safely home again."

"Bless her crazy heart," Marianne said. "She's a chip right off the old block."

"Off me!" Her father yanked away the confining necktie as he started upstairs to change for dinner. "That's base slander. Compared to Andy, I'm a rock-bound conservative."

By the time her mother reached home Andy had the foldboat completely knocked down and packed into its two bags. The one with shoulder straps for back-carrying looked like a fat sack of potatoes. The other, which contained the long pieces of wood, was rather like a golf bag. She was just kneeing the last chair into place when she saw her mother standing in the doorway of the living room, her little face almost hidden behind an armful of country flowers. Mother looked gay as a cricket this evening. She always came home in a sprightly mood after a day with the "girls." "Graying fast but girls forever," she said when the family teased her about the word.

"Hello, my pet," Mother called. "What have you been up to all day?"

"My boat came," Andy said, stars in her eyes.

"The foldboat?"

"What else? I've been all afternoon putting it together."

"But you've done that dozens of times."

"Never *my* boat." Magic hovered about the words as Andy spoke them. "Never all alone."

"Fun?"

Andy grabbed her mother around the neck and hugged her. "Oh, honestly, Mother. If this trip to Lodore doesn't hurry up and come I'm going to explode. I'm so excited I hurt inside."

"Darling, look out! The roses! You'll mash them to jelly." Mother laid the flowers on the hall table and her hands caught Andy on each side of her face. "Let me look at you. You *are* excited. You'll wear yourself out before you ever get started."

"But, Mother, you don't know. Nobody knows—nobody could possibly understand what it means to me to be *able* to do this. It's—it's . . ." Her voice failed completely.

"I think we understand, darling. Dad and I. Some of it anyhow. Which is why we're willing to have you go. And now how about shifting out of those shorts into a dress for dinner? A pretty one."

"Oh, *Mother*." The lighted look on Andy's face damped out.

"Please, darling. The new apple-green plaid I sent home for you last week."

Andy's golden-brown eyes looking straight into her mother's gray ones said, "All right. For you I'll do it." But her voice was lost in her throat, and her thoughts were far away on the white water rushing down between the cliffs of Lodore.

CHAPTER TWO

When Andy was two years old she had urgently demanded of her parents, "Wanta go on a mountain."
The mountain was Tamalpais, which reared its head
nearly three thousand feet into the air across the bay
from the Dawson house. She had started going on the
mountain at the age of two months cradled in a Bergen
knapsack on her father's back. When she could sit up
she graduated to a chair rig. There she waved her short
fat legs and peered out from under the brim of an enormous straw hat. By the time Andrea was four she
could cover trail with a sure-footedness that an older
child might have envied.

Marianne did not envy it in the least. Like all the
Dawson children, she had spent many bright Sundays
with her parents walking the ridge trails or redwood
canyons of Marin County. But by the time Marianne
was six she began to beg off. She preferred to play with
dolls under the eye of a sitter, visit her grandparents,
anything, rather than trudge up and down hill under
her own power.

But Andy never tired of the mountain. Her sturdy
legs raced ahead, her brown eyes danced, while her
hair turned lemon color under the summer sun.

In school Andy was first out on the jungle gym at recess. When another girl did something hard on the rings or bars she had to do it in a way that was a little harder. The fact that her competitor might be older or bigger did not count at all with Andy.

Away from the cemented city, she looked for trees to climb. If anyone said, "Dare you to jump off that next branch," Andy jumped. Always she had to be first, climb highest, jump farthest, run the fastest.

Over the years she managed to take a good deal of skin off her body by doing these things. In fact her mother used to say that any day Andy came home from school without a new Band-Aid deserved special celebration. But basically she seemed indestructible. She fell, but like a cat, landed right side up.

After school she roller-skated down San Francisco's precipitous hills, scuffed her knees, came home to be patched up, and went out to do it over again. She learned to balance on a borrowed bicycle several sizes too large while her older sister was still pedaling contentedly on three wheels.

When Andy was six her father took her skiing. And that was the beginning of a passion. "Snow-flying," she called it, squealing gleefully, "Look, Daddy! I'm Peter Pan!" Complete lack of fear, sturdy muscles, and rare co-ordination made her a natural for the sport.

Mother was never very fond of skiing. She insisted the only pleasant part of this winter pastime was that it felt so good to stop. Marianne hated the cold. When she fell down, which was about every five minutes, she refused to move again until every particle of snow had been brushed from her mittens and clothes. In the course of a morning this became quite an operation. When Skeeter was old enough he went along to look over the cars on the highway. But his heart was not in the highlands. Andy was the one who could scarcely wait from one weekend to the next.

Gradually the winter pattern of the Dawson family emerged. Andy and her father headed for the Sierra by themselves. For Andy, weekends were far too short. The days between dragged slow as an oxcart.

She looked forward to the children's ski school during Easter vacation more eagerly than to Christmas. And the best part of ski school was the races at the end of it.

"Why don't you wait till next year to go into the Easter-egg hunt?" her father suggested. "The snow's mighty slick today."

Andy stamped her chunky ski boot and cried, "No! Now! I'm going to find the most Easter eggs of anybody."

Soon after her ninth birthday she passed the fourth-class test. She could now snowplow to a stop, do a kick turn, side-slip, and perform four linked stem turns under perfect control. With an expression half humorous, half tender, the big man bent down to pin the emblem which was her reward on his daughter.

"Do you still think races are the best part of skiing, Andy?" he asked.

"I'll say."

"Why do you?"

"Why? Oh, I don't know. It's so much fun to beat somebody. It sort of helps you to know if you're any good or not."

"You're good, Andy. That's what bothers me. You're too good for your age. First thing you know you'll be through with the junior races and wanting to enter the senior women's races. You'll be asking to go to Aspen in January and Sun Valley in February and——"

"Dad, I *won't*. You're an old silly."

On Easter Sunday two years later Dr. Dawson stood with the club pro watching the finish of the junior sla-

lom as Andy came into sight, bending almost to the
snow between the gates.

The stocky Norwegian turned to her father. "She
cannot win this year. But next year, when Pat Fair-
banks is no longer a junior . . ."

Dr. Dawson's voice rang rich with pride as he answered, "The child has an instinct for it, doesn't she?"

A glint came into the ice-blue eyes of the instructor
as he gestured toward the flying scarlet jacket. "There,"
he said, "comes championship material."

Almost fiercely Erick Dawson turned on his daughter's teacher. "Who wants a champion? Let her have
fun here on the hill. If she goes into big-time compet-
itive skiing she'll kill herself trying to outdo people
twice her age."

"Hah! Not that Andy! Such co-ordination I have
never seen in a girl so young."

"I know my daughter. For her to be second is disaster."

The following year Andy did win the junior slalom.
She also won the downhill race. From first snowfall in
the Sierra until spring sunshine melted the pack she
studied the weather reports avidly. When her father
could not leave for the weekend she wangled a ride
with someone else. During the week she sat on the din-
ing-room table wiggling her ankles to strengthen them,
did knee bends every morning before breakfast. The beginning, middle, and end of life was skiing.

And skiing led directly to knowing Don. For him, too,
the smell of ski wax was the best perfume in the world.
For him, too, going out on the boards was the biggest
thrill on earth. For a long time Andy and Don had
seen each other scrambling up and down the club hills,
riding the rope tow. She knew his name, he knew hers.
They said "Hi, Andy," and "Hi, Don," as they passed.

But he never really stood out from the swarm of other
boys scurrying around in the snow.

Then suddenly, on the hot September day when she
entered junior high school, there sat Don in her home
room. He grinned and waved. Andy waved back. It
was a warm and wonderful feeling. In this new school,
more than half full of strangers, they were old friends.
They both knew things that nobody else in the class
knew. They shared a special language—corn snow, pow-
der, stem turn, Christy. For most of their friends those
words were meaningless as Chinese. But for Andy and
Don they were the very core of existence. All of life re-
volved around two long wooden boards and a pair of
stainless-steel poles.

That winter they found themselves in the same danc-
ing-school class on Friday afternoons. "Do you like
dancing, Andy?" Don asked as he yanked her out onto
the floor and thrust an arm around her waist.

"I certainly don't," Andy said. "The thing I hate most,
though, is those white gloves we have to wear to class.
But Mother says I'll feel awfully dumb later on if I
don't learn to dance while I'm young."

Don chuckled. "Your mother and mine must have
been reading the same book."

"Maybe when skiing gets good we can skip dancing
school once in a while for a longer weekend," Andy
suggested hopefully.

Don's scrubbed face looked gloomy. "My mother says
I have to go to dancing school for at least a year—reg-
ularly—or no skiing. Gosh, what a gyp! Why do they
have to have the darn thing on Fridays? There are four
other days in the week. All useless."

Snow fell late in the mountains that year, melted off,
and fell again thinly. It was a miserable ski season. The
resort owners along highway 40 moaned about going
out of business. Don and Andy shared their anguish,

hoping, watching, waiting, fuming at the endless days
of sunshine. When at last a fair snow pack had fallen,
they both rushed into skiing as if there would never be
another chance in their lives to go flying down that
white track between the pines.

Six months ago these two had been just names to
each other. Now they were firm friends with that best
of all bases for friendship, joy in doing the same thing.
When skiing was out of season they went on picnics
together, served on school committees. Andy helped
Don with social studies, which he hated; he helped her
untangle problems in arithmetic. But for both of them
skiing was all that really mattered.

By the time they entered the ninth grade Andy was
known around school as Don's girl. It embarrassed her
a little. Still it was a good feeling—a proudish feeling.
Don was a guy to be proud *of*. He was no big athletic
hot shot, but he was always being chairman of something or other. Student council, traffic court, things like
that. No matter what Don did he seemed to get to the
top. His wide-awake face was easy to look at and even
in jeans he looked as if he had just come out of a shower
where he had used soap and a nailbrush with all his
might. His brisk crew cut was as far removed as possible
from the greasy brushed-back locks worn by a few of
the boys at school.

Andy was always surprised at how many people Don
knew. Not only in their own class, but seventh and
eighth graders too. He remembered their names and was
never too wound up in his own affairs to say "Hi" as
he breezed down the corridor.

Also, Andy thought, it's nice to know that at parties
I'll never be a wallflower. Not while Don's around.

For Christmas that year Don gave her a present. Because it was the first time he had ever done so she had
no gift for him, but secretly she vowed that next year

she would give Don some wonderful surprise. Maybe she'd learn to knit and make him a pair of ski socks. For a long time Andy remembered every detail of that Christmas morning. Far longer than she wanted to remember it.

About ten o'clock Don rode over on his bike. Andrea was in the middle of trying on a new blue sweater, one arm in and one arm out, when she saw him through the front window. Don was taller than Andy now. Just this year he seemed to have shot up like bamboo. All in one motion he swung his leg over the back wheel and leaned the bicycle against the house. When the doorbell rang Andy raced to open the front door, to be the first to shout, "Merry Christmas."

As Don came in, the living room was still a jumble of colored wrappings and streamers of ribbon and shredded-up tissue paper from the box in which Mother's new crystal goblets had been packed.

"Hi, everybody!" Don called out. "Merry Christmas!" He lifted his big feet high, stepping over packages and papers until he stood in the middle of the room.

Skeeter was down on his knees under the Christmas tree pushing a model sports car round and round to see if the wheels moved exactly the way wheels moved on a real sports car. Marianne was playing her new album of the *Gondoliers* at top volume.

Skeeter got up from his knees and yelled, "Merry Christmas, Don." Marianne turned off the record player. Everybody was delighted that Don had come over.

After all the merry Christmases had been said Don fished into his pocket and brought out a little box. "Catch, Andy," he said, tossing it to her halfway across the room. She reached up and caught it neatly on the fly. "Brought you a little something for luck. Wear it when you go into your next race. Will you?"

Absurdly Andy felt her hands shaking as she untied

the scarlet ribbon. Under the top layer of cotton was a
tiny silver lapel pin in the shape of a pair of skis.

"Why, Don!" she cried, feeling as if several frogs had
lodged in her throat. "Why, Don—how—how absolutely
terrific. Of course I'll wear it when I race. I bet with
this I'll beat everybody in sight." Proudly she fastened
it to the collar of her dress.

"Glad you like it, Andy." Don's face glistened with
pleasure as he watched her.

"Like it? I'm feeble about it. Thanks, Don. Thank
you just ever and *ever* so much."

Andy wore Don's pin not only when she skied. She
also wore it on coats and sweaters and dresses, and if
Marianne had not shared her room she would have worn
it on the lapel of her pajamas. But Marianne would
laugh at that—or at least smile in a superior way—and
being laughed at was a thing Andy could not endure.
The pin became her most precious possession. It stood
for skiing and winning, and for all the fun of being Don's
girl.

Black Saturday came late in March. It wasn't even
a race. She was just out on the hill practicing. It was one
of those things that couldn't happen but did.

Andy remembered seeing the dark blue body hurtling
toward her out of control, remembered leaning desperately to swerve out of the way. She remembered the
boy's voice, harsh with terror, screaming, "Tra-ack!"
Then the world exploded. There was a splintering crack
of wood, clouds of snow muffling her breath, white-hot
knives stabbing up and down her left leg.

She tried to move, fell back again, blurry with pain.
"I've broken my leg," she mumbled dully, staring up
at the tree against which she was wedged. "I'll be
grounded all the rest of the year." Once more she tried

to struggle up, to unfold the leg which was bent under her body. Waves of agony blanked out thought.

After a time hands lifted her onto a sled and Andy dug her fingernails into her palms to keep from screaming as they brought her down the slope.

"Dad—where's Dad?" she gasped, opening her eyes to look for the face which had always made the world so safe.

A strange voice answered. "He'll be along pretty soon, Andy. He's skiing over at Sugarbowl today. They've gone to get him."

Another doctor was at the lodge. He jabbed a needle into her arm, and when at last she did see her father's face bending over her in the bunk she was almost too drowsy to care.

Getting back to the city, being wheeled through the bleak hospital corridors and put to bed remained forever a haze of pain and unknown faces.

The first days after surgery were full of physical misery, but still in a way they were exciting. There were flowers popping in at all hours from aunts and uncles and friends. Don sent a big bunch of daffodils and blue Dutch iris which she made the nurse put on the bedside table—even when she insisted there was no room. Andy wanted Don's flowers where she could reach out every little while to feel their smooth cool petals. There was a clean garden fragrance about them too, which reminded her of Don.

Each mail brought letters or get-well-quickly cards from girls at school, and some of Mother's and Dad's friends sent presents—books, toilet water, delicious-smelling soap. Every day was Christmas. Mother kept a list of all the gifts so that when Andy felt better she could write notes to thank the people who had tried to make her accident easier to bear.

More than a week went by before they let Don come

to see her in the hospital. And when at last he came
they were both a little embarrassed. It seemed completely goofy to be lying down talking to Don. He stood
awkwardly beside the high bed while he told about the
skiing he had done last week. Then he wandered
around the room, examined the roll-up cranks at the
foot of the bed, and finally lighted way off in a big chair
by the window. Then neither of them could think of
another word to say.

"How's school?" Andy asked finally, more to break
the queer silence than because she really wanted to
know. Already school seemed part of another life.

"Same as ever," Don said. "Hope the snow lasts till
Easter vacation, but nobody thinks it will."

She dreamed up a few more questions and Don answered them before he pulled up again onto his gangly
legs. "Gosh, Andy, I guess I better not stay too long.
I don't want to tire you out or anything."

"Oh, Don, I'm not tired. It's wonderful seeing you
again. Hearing about skiing and everything."

"Well, anyway—I'd better be on my horse. Be seeing
you." He vanished into the dark maw of the hospital
hall. Walking, just walking easily and quickly on two
legs, began to seem a miraculous thing.

After a few more days the flowers stopped coming.
And the presents. The river of cards and letters became
a trickle. Don's visits, also, grew farther and farther
apart. The last time he came to the hospital Andy had
graduated into a wheel chair on the roof garden. He
strode up to her through the spattered sunshine—how
easily he moved across the floor—stood putting his hands
in and out of his pockets in an unnatural sort of way.
Curious for Don to be ill at ease.

"How's the leg, Andy?" He didn't wait for her to answer. "Sorry I haven't been around to see you for so
long. Been busy as heck the last few days. You sort of

have to keep in the swim of things if you want to get
to the top of the heap."

"How do you mean, Don?"

"Well, everybody does. Men in business. Guys in college. Everybody's on his way up. If nobody ever sees
you——" He stopped short, realizing the implications of
what he was saying.

"You might as well be in a hospital," Andy said. But
she did not smile as she said it.

"Aw—Andy. I didn't mean that. But I've got the
lead in the graduation play, and what with learning
the lines and all——" He stammered a little. "Th-those
rehearsals take up an awful lot of time after school too."

Andy said, "I hope I can see you in the play. By June
I ought to be practically well."

"Sure you will be, by June. That'll be swell, Andy."

"Dad and the orthopedist who takes care of me both
say I have to be terribly patient, though. Besides breaking my leg bones it seems I tore up the ligaments in a
really big way. That's what the operation was for, to
stitch the ligaments back where they belong. Ligaments
take forever to get strong again."

Don looked away from Andrea's strained face, staring out across the ugly roofs and chimney tops of the
city below them. "Seems funny not to be graduating together, the way we've always talked about it. All those
good ninth-grade parties we were going to take in at
the end of school."

It was on the tip of Andrea's tongue to ask, "Who's
giving parties?" But something held her back, some
oddness in Don's face. A curtain had fallen between
them. She and Don were friends—sure—good old friends.
But she knew as clearly as if he had told her so that
minute that she had stopped being Don's special girl.
Not Cinderella's coach and all the footmen, she thought,
could drag me to that class play.

As soon as she was able to manage crutches they let
her go home from the hospital. That was a thrill at first.
Home food, all her favorite food, the whole house to
roam about in, the family together in the evenings.
But time soon began to drag even more than it had in
the hospital. Everyone she knew, even her own family,
seemed to be busy all day long. Mother found a tutor
to help her make up the schoolwork she had lost, but
Andy could not seem to concentrate on lessons. Don
telephoned once or twice, said he was rehearsing madly,
no time to come over. Then the calls stopped.

Father said, "Let her drop back six months, do the
high ninth over again. What difference does it make?"

Mother said, "But she's so bored all day. And she'll
hate starting high school a term behind her old gang.
Wouldn't you, Andy?"

Andy shrugged and turned away. "I don't know. I
don't know what I want. Just to be able to walk again,
I guess, and get my muscles into shape for skiing next
winter."

The tutor was dropped. For a time Andy tried to
busy herself painting. She puttered with finger painting, water colors, pastels. Splashing around in poster
paints like mud pies was fun, but her heart was not in
it. Painting was not a game, not something you could
win. As a matter of fact, her heart was in moth balls.
She had packed it away very carefully where nothing
could get at it, where nothing could hurt it. She thought
nothing could hurt it, but the worst blow came later.

The shredded ligaments on each side of her knee
healed slowly. She learned to walk without crutches.
But the great orthopedic surgeon said she could not
ski.

"Not ski? You mean not ski all winter?" Andy's
voice suggested that she had been asked not to eat
all winter.

"I mean not ski, Andrea, my dear. Not this winter—
or ever. That knee is going to be unstable—always. You
must be careful of it for a long, long time. If you wrench
it again . . ." The doctor's face wore that calm un-
emotional mask physicians put on to tell their patients
unpleasant truths. "Well—don't let it happen."

All that had gone before was childish grief compared
to this. Always before there was hope. There would be
a time—sometime—a future when she would be well
again, when she would ski. This was the end of the
world.

Her father took her not to one orthopedic surgeon,
but to three, before giving up. The answer was always
the same. The knee would be permanently unstable.
A good enough knee to get around on, walk on, perhaps
even dance on eventually. But skiing, with control cen-
tered in the knees—no. Skiing was out—forever. In the
doctor's office Andy sat dry-eyed, biting her lips, twisting her fingers behind her back. But her pillow had
streaks on it in the morning—many mornings.

When Marianne came home from college she said,
"Why don't you take up the piano? It would open new
worlds to you. I'll get you started."

Andy scoffed. "In the first place I'm as musical as a
chimpanzee. And in the second place I'd never catch
up with *you*."

"Why would catching up with me matter? I'll never
catch up with Myra Hess."

"Well, it would." The stubborn jaw clamped shut and
she went off by herself to wrestle with this strange new
antagonist, time. Too much time.

The following January she graduated from junior
high. But school no longer had any flavor. She drudged
through the days, instead of moving as a vital cog,
knowing her place. The thought of high school filled
her with dread, but she was too proud to admit it. In

high school girls had dates. You had to have dates or you were weird. And Andy didn't want any dates. She didn't want anything to do with the whole silly business.

Not even to herself did Andy admit that she was plain scared. Afraid some other boy would invite her out half a dozen times, then drop her like an empty beer can tossed out on the highway. Instead she told herself that being a girl and being obliged to sit around waiting until some boy asked you to go somewhere was a stupid convention. There was nothing you could do about it. No way to win. You were competing, but not openly. The only answer was to avoid boys entirely. This she told herself so often that she finally came to believe it.

"I don't intend to sit around the house jumping every time the telephone rings," she said scornfully to Marianne. "And I don't want to get done up in a date dress or have to put my hair up in bobby pins every night or go through all the other rigamarole girls go through to make boys like them." Andy's chin went up in the air as she spoke. She much preferred to wear jeans every moment she was not in school and not be bothered with boys.

What she did want, Andy had no idea until she met Chuck Tormey.

CHAPTER THREE

No one had ever described Charles Tormey as a walking dream. Doubtless no one ever would. A hard-muscled wisp of a man with thinning hair and squirrel-bright eyes in his freckled face, he was, nevertheless, the most popular teacher in the vast milling high school where Andrea tried to pick up the threads of living. In class he was, of course, Mr. Tormey. But outside he was Chuck.

Long before she elected biology Andy knew Chuck's reputation. Knew that girls who entered his class ready to squeal at the sight of a worm ended talking about "my frog" with downright affection. It was Chuck Tormey's own passionate excitement over the small miracles to be found in all living matter which lighted up the dry bones of science for his students. That, plus the sure knowledge that in him they had a friend. For to this man without wife or children of his own, all the boys and girls he taught were his children. To help them, nothing was too much trouble.

Some girls chose Chuck's biology course because of the weekend trips where there were always more boys than girls. While they walked, they hunted and fished —though not always for forest or marine specimens. But Andy huddled with other girls or played it alone. She was the girl, she told herself, who was different. The girl who was bored by boys.

It was on a Saturday field trip to one of the unfrequented beaches north of San Francisco that she first found herself spilling her life history to Chuck. He had led the group on a rough scramble over wet rocks laid bare by low tide. As they straggled along, sniffing seaweed, poking into crannies between rocks, he rambled on about the amazing way in which ingenious little marine creatures had learned to live either underwater at high tide or out of it at low.

Still afraid to trust her weak knee, Andy hung back from the roughest part of the climb. Returning, Chuck found her sitting alone on a driftwood log, looking out across the water with eyes that did not really see. Quickly he scooped her up into his orbit.

"Tired, Andrea?"

"Oh no! Just——" She hesitated, reluctant as always to admit there was something physical she could not do. "It's my knee."

"Well, hey—why didn't you speak up sooner? We always carry an ace bandage in the first-aid kit." Already he had one arm out of his rucksack strap.

"Oh, this didn't happen today. It's a permanent knee. Getting stronger—slowly—but——"

Then, without quite knowing how, Chuck had the whole story out of her. The accident, her feeling about skiing, the way as a small girl she had called it snow-flying. And flying it still was in memory, as close as a person could come to heaven.

As she talked to Chuck other memories of winter days came crowding back. The pungent smell of ski wax, the hum of the rope tow, blue shadows on the snow as the jay-bar jolted past dark pine trees bent with white, ice-edged wind nipping the tops of her ears, the comfort of the warming hut—and Don. A whole flood of pic-

tures rushed in at the thought of Don. But these she
pushed quickly to the very bottom of her mind and did
not mention to Chuck at all.

"Perhaps I'll be able to water-ski someday," she
finished, reaching for a laugh to smother the tears which
had come dangerously near the surface as she let
thoughts of skiing come to life again. "I've seen pictures of people doing that on one leg."

Chuck didn't sympathize with Andy. He didn't say
anything at all just then. Merely turned his head a few
inches so that she felt his quick eyes studying her as
if she were a specimen under the microscope.

It was not until after they had eaten their sand-
wiches, stuffed the wax paper and orange peelings back
into their knapsacks, and settled into the sand for a
short rest that Chuck came up with his suggestion. The
suggestion which revolutionized Andy's life.

"Been thinking about you, Andrea. Why don't you
take up foldboating? It's the nearest thing there is to
skiing."

"Foldboating! What's that?"

"Riding round in a foldboat, naturally." Chuck
plucked off his visored cap to let the breeze sweeping
in over the Pacific ruffle the few hairs which still remained on the top of his head. Unsheltered, his eyes
bored directly into Andy's eyes. "It's quite a sport, my
friend. Not to be picked up in a weekend any more
than skiing is."

"But where? How do you start?"

"On a river, in the bay. In winter we start 'em in a
swimming pool."

Andy looked incredulous. "Chuck, you're kidding.
So I go to my father and say, 'Dad, I'd like a fold-up
boat, please. I plan to take a run up the Sacramento
River next week.'"

A gnomish grin stretched Chuck's mouth. "It's much

simpler than that. If you want to give the thing a whirl you can come out with me. I have a double foldboat. Holds two. But you'll have to promise two things."

"Such as?"

Suddenly Chuck exploded with a startled "You do swim, don't you?"

"Heavens yes. Quite well really."

"Okay then. That I should have asked first. Now— as I was saying. Number one, promise to call it a fold-boat, not a fold-up boat. And second, don't talk about traveling *up* the Sacramento. The idea is to let the current do the work while you guide the boat."

"Doesn't sound too hard."

Chuck snorted. "Live and learn. Come out a week from tomorrow and meet some of the other River Runners. We're having an easy one-day trip on the Russian River. You can be a passenger if you like, or start handling a paddle. Ever canoe?"

"I've ridden in one a time or two along the edge of Lake Tahoe. Never paddled. It certainly didn't feel anything like skiing. I nearly went to sleep."

Chuck took a breath of clean ocean air deep into his lungs, let it out again slowly. "A-ahh! Wait till you hit white water." And in the words "white water" Andy sensed a spark of excitement she herself had not felt since before Black Saturday.

All week long she wondered about foldboating, edgy with anticipation, nervous about how she would perform. Certainly she had no idea of being just a passenger.

The whole family was delighted to have her go. Skeeter put it more frankly than the others when he said, "I sure hope this foldboat deal takes. Maybe then you'll stop moping around the house every weekend."

Early Sunday morning while Mother was still asleep Andy and her father cooked up a quick kitchen breakfast. Skeeter, barefoot in his pajamas, stumbled in on them, still rubbing sleep out of his eyes.

" 'By, Andy," he mumbled. "Hope you have fun." Then, gathering up a handful of graham crackers, he went back to spread crumbs around his bed.

Through the gray morning mist Dad drove her to Chuck Tormey's house, where she met her first foldboat and the first of the River Runners.

"Morning, Andy," Chuck called as they drove up. With another man he was busy fastening an already set up foldboat onto the roof of his car. He did not come to meet Dr. Dawson until they had it finally secured.

A tall girl with a knot of straight blond hair pinned at her neck stood on the sidewalk watching the two men. She stepped forward, holding out a firm brown hand. "I'm Liz Monkton," she said. "And I know you are Andrea Dawson."

Andy said, "Hello," and introduced her father.

"That carrottop helping Chuck," Liz went on, "is my husband. You might as well start calling him Monk because he won't answer to anything else. He purely detests his real name."

"Something like Nebuchadnezzar?" Andy suggested.

But before Liz could answer, a battered little Volkswagen pulled up at the curb and a string-bean youth unfolded himself from the front seat, dragging a knapsack and two boat bags after him.

"Here's Connie Van Fleet," Liz announced. "Now we can push off. He's our fifth passenger. We always fill up the cars for river trips. Gas is such an item. At least in *our* budget it is." The smile she turned on Dr. Dawson made it quite clear that there was no budget for happiness in Liz Monkton's life.

Chuck Tormey and Monk joined them then. How-do-you-do's spilled about and Andy knew from the look on her father's face that he at once liked Chuck. She

was glad of that. Dad was not one to be deceived by
a scrawny exterior.

She was glad, too, that as he said good-by her father
did not go all parental, as Mother might have done,
and say, "Take good care of my little girl," or warn
them about her knee. Maybe foldboating would be dull
and hateful. But if she did like it, if it really was like
skiing, she wanted these new friends to think of her as
whole and competent. Cute old Dad, she thought, giving him a little salute with one finger as he drove down
the street.

As she turned back to the group on the sidewalk Andrea zipped up her windbreaker right to the neck to shut
out the bite of fog and wind. The jacket was tight across
the shoulders now. Still it was good to be wearing it
again even if the pants below were denim jeans instead
of tapered wool.

On the drive to Russian River, Andrea decided to
listen hard and say little. Liz and Monk, she soon
gleaned from the chatter, had been married only a couple of months. Monk was evidently a seasoned foldboater and was working hard to bring his wife out of
the green-pea class. The moment they became engaged
he sold his boat to buy a double one. But even with
such devoted tuition Liz claimed she wouldn't dare go
out alone.

Connie Van Fleet rode in the front seat with Chuck.
Seen in profile, Connie's angular face looked so much
like a horse that Andy half expected to hear a whinny
come out of it. Instead, he spoke in a gentle high-pitched
voice that matched his gentle handshake.

"Where do we put in?" Connie inquired. "Healdsburg?"

"That's right. You must have read your bulletin this
month," Chuck added dryly.

Andy made a quick mental note. "Put in." That must

be River Runner lingo for put the boat in the water.

"Probably seem a touch tropical up there to you—after pneumonia gulch," Chuck teased.

Connie accepted the ribbing cheerfully. He was a student at San Francisco State College, on the edge of the ocean, and he was quite used to jokes about the fog which hovered over his alma mater.

"Two more carloads are meeting us at Healdsburg," Chuck went on. "While the boats are being set up we'll shuttle the cars down to Monte Rio. Meanwhile Monk or somebody can give Andrea a start on the facts of foldboating. How to get in, how to hold a paddle. Or would you rather just go for the ride today?"

"Certainly not. I want to learn."

"Atta girl," Liz said. "It'll be warm up there, so Chuck won't mind if you dump him in the river a time or two."

"Oh, I'll try not to do *that*," Andrea said, her face taut with worry.

A pleasant laugh rippled around the car at her intensity. "Don't give it a thought." Monk gave her a fatherly pat on the shoulder. "Half of foldboating is falling in the water. In fact one of the first things you need to learn is how to upset gracefully."

"We have another brand-new beginner today," Chuck told them. "Martha Frayne is bringing her son."

"I've never seen Tim," Liz said. "How old a boy is he?"

"Just eleven." Chuck spoke slowly, as if he were considering a problem. "Martha has tried any number of times to get him out with her, but he's always refused. He's a brilliant kid, but on the timid side physically."

"My hat's off to that Martha Frayne," Monk said with conviction.

Though she had resolved to be a listener today, Monk's earnestness brought a quick "Why?" out of Andy.

"Well, life hasn't been exactly jam for Martha. Her husband walked out on her before Tim was a year old. She's supported the boy all his life—though lots of women do that of course. I guess mostly my hat's off to her because of what she is. Martha seems to get a kick out of just being alive. No self-pity, always a hand out to help the other fellow, and wonderful fun to have around."

As they rolled over the Golden Gate Bridge and northward through the rounded hills of Marin County, Andy let Monk's description of Martha Frayne filter through her mind. A good recipe, she decided, for a personality. Never sorry for herself, a ready hand for the other fellow, and fun to have around. Martha sounded nice.

In late spring the Russian River ran bank full at Healdsburg. Nevertheless, it was a pastoral-looking stream. At least there were no riffles or rocks in sight. The other cars were already parked at the trysting spot below the bridge, and Andy noticed a woman and a boy paddling slowly close to shore. Martha Frayne and Tim, she was sure, but Monk gave her no time to watch them.

"Come on, Andy," he said, handing her a knapsack to carry. "Chuck and those other two drivers won't be back from the car shuttle for at least an hour and a half. I'll initiate you." He carried the two bags containing the Monkton boat to a stretch of gravelly beach, left his wife to grapple with the problem of setting it up.

"But I never in my life did this all alone," Liz wailed as Monk loped away with Andy in tow.

"You couldn't start any younger," he called over his shoulder. "Don't worry, Liz. I'll be back long before those shuttlers are. If you get stuck just wait for me."

Monk picked up one end of Chuck's boat, indicated that Andy was to carry the other end. "Since this is

your maiden voyage in a foldboat, I think I'll get in first.
They're tippy contraptions till you get the hang of
them." He laughed ruefully. "My bounding bride put
us both in the drink on *her* first try. The heavier person
usually sits in back to give the nose of the boat a chance
to rise over the waves."

"If any," Andy said, devoutly hoping there would
not be any today.

As he talked Monk screwed together the two halves
of a double-bladed paddle, showed Andy how to
grasp it, hands on top, thumbs underneath. "The water
is barely waist-deep right here, so let's skip the life preserver for now. We better put the spray deck on, though.
You may heave a paddle full of water onto your lap."

The spray deck was a waterproof affair which gathered close around Andy's waist and fastened to the
coaming. Then Monk eased the boat into the water and
climbed in.

"Ready?"

Andy nodded. Her heart was thudding against her
ribs as if she were about to schuss down a perpendicular
mountain of snow.

"First screw your paddle together. There are different ways of setting the blades, but no need to go into
that today. Now lay the paddle across the bow and
step in. Put your foot on the wooden part." He kept
the boat from drifting by holding to a branch of willow
on the bank, but the expected lurch did not come.

"Good girl. Nice balance." The warm surprise in
Monk's voice gave Andy a genuine thrill. "Now brace
your knees on those places where Chuck has pads of
foam rubber and your feet against one of the wooden
ribs down under the bow."

Andy did as she was told, then looked around at her
instructor.

"All set?"

She jerked her head, not daring to trust her voice. "Here we go then."

It was an odd feeling to be sitting on the bottom of the boat, below water level really. I'm almost a part of the river, she thought, picking up the paddle to wait for Monk's directions.

"Your left arm should go to a full stretch before you lift the blade out of the water. Then push on your right. That's the stuff. Push on the blade that's up in the air. If you keep using a bent arm to *pull* the paddle through the water you'll be worn to a nubbin in no time."

Slowly, smoothly, they moved along the edge of the bank. Monk showed her how to turn the bow by paddling forward with one blade, back-paddling with the other.

"Something about this makes me feel like a swan," Andy said hesitantly.

"Why a swan, for Pete's sake? I've always thought swans were the stuffed shirts of the bird family."

"I don't know *why*, Monk. Perhaps because it feels so glidey. And swans never seem to be actually swimming through the water. They just sail over the top by magic."

Monk chuckled. "That's because I'm doing all the work for you." To prove it, he shipped his paddle for a moment. Instantly the little craft slewed about in the current which was stronger than it looked to an unpracticed eye. The boat began to rock. Andy paddled with all her might, but they only rocked harder.

"Hold your body still," Monk ordered. "Your arm and shoulder muscles are supposed to do the work. Not your whole back."

In a moment she felt the foldboat swing back again parallel to the current, and the swanlike glide resumed.

"I see what you mean, Monk," she said humbly. "I wasn't really paddling at all."

"You're doing beautifully. Chuck will be as pleased as a mother hen with a new chick."

Monk's nice, Andy thought. Easy to talk to. Why aren't boys my own age like this? She flicked the thought away and put her whole mind as well as her whole energy into paddling.

Skeeter got his wish about foldboating. Like a good vaccination, it did take and Andy no longer spent her weekends wondering what to do. The infatuation did not happen all at once. That first day on the Russian River she enjoyed herself enough to want more. But it was her first taste of white water some weeks later on the Feather River that turned Andy into an addict.

"It isn't every new foldboater I'd take down this run," Chuck told her as they walked back along the edge of the river after scouting the rocks and rapids ahead. "But I'll take you, Andy, because you can take directions. Also, I know you won't lose your head and panic on me."

When they were seated in the boat again Andy braced her feet rigidly, her mind aquiver to remember every detail she had worked to learn. They moved out into the current.

Suddenly there was a roar of water in her ears. "Submerged rock on your left," Chuck shouted as they rounded a bend. The lashing water ahead looked utterly impassable. The river grabbed the boat and they were flying through the waves at breathless speed.

"Lean backward—NOW——" Chuck bellowed. The nose of the boat rose in the air, dropped hard into a hole below the rock. White spray drenched them. She was drowned in water.

"Oh, Chuck, it *is*," Andrea squealed at the top of her voice. "It *is* like skiing."

It did not matter that the words were lost in the crash of water. The ecstasy of speed was flowing in her veins again. This was "water-flying." Beyond the limits and possibilities of the human body. This was IT!

It was a short rapid and as they coasted into calm water at the end of it Andy turned around with a quick smile for the man who had unlocked for her a new door to heaven.

"Like it?" he asked, squinting his eyes against the sun.

"*Like* it? Oh, Chuck——" she whispered. And could think of nothing more to say. She wanted to throw her arms around him, dance wildly, leap in the air, do something utterly mad to express the way she felt. It was like coming to life again after being dead.

"Is there more white water like this?" she asked finally.

"There's more, Andy." Chuck's own voice was suspiciously husky. "More coming today and more white water in America than you and I could run in all our lives."

CHAPTER FOUR

During the next two years Andrea Dawson became a really skillful foldboater. This was not accidental. She worked at it with all the passion she had once lavished on skiing. She read foldboating, thought foldboating, and week after week she went out with Chuck to paddle the rivers of California. The American, the Truckee, the Stanislaus, the Tuolumne, the Merced, the mild and the treacherous—mile by mile she came to familiarity with them all.

Because she was so busy with river touring, certain squirming memories were covered up in Andrea's mind. She no longer thought of the night during her first term at high school when Lew Davis took her to his club formal. She had not wanted to go, but Mother urged so hard she finally gave in. It was the first time since Black Saturday that Andy had tried to dance. Out of practice and pitifully conscious of her weak knee, they stumbled over each other's feet. Lew apologized and turned red. Andy grew totally tongue-tied. Lew tried to teach her a new step, but she was unable to follow him. She longed to disappear, thought of hiding in the coat closet till the music stopped. But sheer stubbornness made her stick it out in spite of sly behind-the-hand giggles which she sensed from other twirling couples.

Lew never called her again, for which Andy was grateful. But for a long time the evening remained an intolerable red coal smoldering at the back of her mind. Evidently Lew passed the word around that a date with Andy Dawson was a date with a clam, because no one else called her either.

Then in the middle of junior year John Percoletti transferred from high school in Elko, Nevada. Promptly he invited Andy to be his partner at the junior Hi-De-Ho on Saturday night.

"Sorry, John," Andy told him. "I'm going foldboating that weekend."

"Foldboating! What's that?"

"It's divine," Andy said, color pinking her cheeks. "You run rapids in a little canvas boat."

"Do you do it often?"

"Every weekend—practically."

"Well, blow me flat!" John said, giving her a look half puzzled and half accusing. "So that's why I never see you around."

"That's why. Thanks just the same, John."

All the way home Andy thought about John's invitation. Perhaps she was foolish to have turned it down. Perhaps she should really try to get in the swim again. John seemed like a nice person, and certainly if she backed out of one or two weekends Chuck would understand. Yet riding the river was a lot more fun. Every time she went out she learned something. These contradictory ideas were still sifting through her head when she let herself in the front door.

Mother was telephoning, and without really meaning to eavesdrop Andy stood frozen in the hall, transfixed by the hurt in her mother's voice.

"Oh, Madge! I'll try. I know it will be a lovely party and I'll use every persuasion short of a stick to get Andy to go. But I know what she'll say. Ever since that accident Andy has shied away from boys her own age as if they were lepers." Mother sounded as if she were ready to cry. "Erick says if we're patient she'll outgrow it. But I don't know. It just doesn't seem normal to me for a pretty, intelligent girl to be that way. Why, at Andrea's age Marianne had the house full of boys all the time. The problem was to keep her from going out too much."

Marianne! Always Marianne! Andy stiffened all over. Could she help it if her sister was little and cute and popular? If she had a quick comeback for every crack? "I'll stick with foldboating. I'll be the best woman foldboater that ever lived," she vowed fiercely. "Those people are my real friends. Age doesn't matter."

Carefully avoiding the creaking side of the third step, Andy tiptoed up to her room. Later, when Mother urged her to go to "the beautiful dance Madge is giving for Dotty's birthday," Andy had her answer ready. "Oh, Mother. I'd only be a closet number and Aunt Madge would be running around all evening trying to bribe people to dance with me. I'd rather go out on the river with Chuck than go to the most marvelous party in the world."

Andrea's steady practice with the paddle paid off. Her muscles grew hard and her skill in handling a boat increased in great leaps.

Chuck was never lavish with praise. But when he mumbled, "Nice going," or "Couldn't have taken that any better myself," Andy glowed. Success was meat and drink to her. And the success she lived for came in a small canvas boat flying through white-crested water.

Occasionally, when Timmie Frayne was busy with his scout troop or just plain refused to come, Andrea shared Martha's double. And she was pleased in her heart when she realized that she was at least as good a foldboater as Martha, who had had years of experience.

In winter she went with a group of River Runners to the tremendous swimming pool at the Alameda Naval Air Base. There, in a bathing suit, she practiced falling out of a boat, righting it, getting in again. She even struggled to learn the Eskimo roll, a maneuver in which the boat turns completely over in the water and comes right side up again without unseating the passenger. The Eskimo roll required great skill and arm strength to pull the paddle through the water. Few girls ever mastered it. But Andy kept trying. It was not just a show-off stunt, but a real rescue technique in a capsizing boat. Also, it was a part of foldboating which was a part of her.

Andrea was pleased, too, to be able to help Finette Reynolds, a beginner Chuck put in her special care. Finette sold clothes in a large department store in the city. She was soft and round and pretty as the dresses she helped other women to buy.

"I've done a lot of canoeing on Minnesota lakes," Finette explained on her first day at the pool. "I thought it might not be too hard to convert one kind of paddle skill into another."

Andy suspected that the canoes in which Finette had ridden were chiefly propelled by tall and handsome on the rear seat. That notion was dispelled, however, within the first hour. Once Finette mastered the rhythm of the double paddle, she was on her way to being a foldboater. Currents and slicks and portages were old hat to her. Working with her was fun, partly because she was lovable as a kitten, even more because it seemed a way of returning some of the patient labor Chuck had invested in Andrea herself.

As the months slipped by, the patter of foldboating,

which had once sounded like a foreign language, became as much a part of Andy as stem turn, Christy, and snowplow had ever been. She chattered about upstream ferry and downstream ferry. She knew which waves were haystacks. *Longeron* was no longer a ten-dollar word. It was just a wooden rib in a boat. She learned to feather her paddles to cut wind resistance, learned the meaning of white patches and slick spots on the surface of the water.

Chuck said she should also learn caution. But that was harder. Like the four-year-old who had raced down the steep trails of Marin County, heedless of spills, something within seemed to drive her full tilt. She had to prove, both to herself and to the world, that she was best. Not just good for her age, but good as anybody—tops. Maybe someday a competitor in the wild Arkansas River race. But Chuck still pounded away on the creed of the River Runners: "Safety comes first."

In October of Andy's second year as a foldboater the group laid plans for a trip on San Francisco Bay from Point Richmond to Angel Island. Paddling in salt water, the old-timers explained, was quite a different kettle of fish from gliding down a river. On the bay the main consideration was the tide.

Mother looked more than a little disturbed when Andy announced at dinner that she might not be home from this Sunday's trip until ten o'clock at night.

"We have to wait for the tide to turn before we can leave Angel Island," she explained, sweeping a hand across her smooth blond hair as if she could already feel the bay wind ruffling it.

Mother gave a little shudder. "I can't bear the thought of your bobbing around the bay in that absurd cockleshell in the pitch-black night. How will you know where you're going?"

"First of all, darling, it won't be pitch-black. There's a full moon come Sunday. And secondly, I will not be alone. I'll be in Chuck's boat and he's done this exact trip twice before. He says it's a breeze compared to running rapids. Takes no skill at all—just a little brute strength to keep on paddling." Andy shoved up the sleeve of her sweater to exhibit the brute strength in her arm.

Mother's gentle gray eyes looked across the table to Father, plainly begging him to say no, just this once, to his crazy daughter. But Father became extremely busy carving more leg of lamb.

With a touch of desperation Mother struggled on. "That Mr. Tormey of yours doesn't look as if he had enough strength to paddle a peanut shell. He's such a wispy little man. Arms and legs like wire."

"Steel wire," Andy said. "You know, it's funny. I never think about what Chuck looks like. The person inside is so terrific that the covering doesn't matter at all. Anyhow, it isn't *really* strength that counts in keeping a boat right side up. It's know-how."

"If you just had a little old motor in your boat, that would be really neat," Skeeter told her.

"If we had a motor it would spoil everything good about foldboating," Andy sputtered. Then they laughed at each other, enjoying and respecting their oppositeness.

From Point Richmond to Angel Island turned out to be a hard four-hour pull. The wind was against them all the way and at times it seemed to Andy that the island was being steadily towed in the opposite direction. When at last they slid in among the sailboats at Hospital Cove she was, for once, truly glad the trip was over.

"I think I'm a fresh-water girl at heart," she said to Chuck as they lifted his boat ashore.

"Shows your good sense."

Andy stretched both arms overhead to relax weary muscles and beamed at the homely freckled face beside her. It was a golden smile, springing straight from the satisfaction that filled her. "We made good time, though. Whit looks like the only person in ahead of us."

"Whit's incredible," Chuck said. "Never seems to exert himself, but always manages to be on exactly the right bit of water at the right moment. Ever notice how rarely he gets into trouble?"

"Guess I'm too busy keeping myself out of trouble," Andrea answered. "What does Whit do, by the way? Besides foldboating every weekend, I mean." For the first time it seemed strange to her that these river friends had lives of their own in which she did not share at all and to whom, in spite of the difference in their ages, she felt more closely bound than to any people in the world except her own family.

"Whit? Why, that old bachelor is a hot-shot stockbroker on Montgomery Street. Your father will have heard of his firm. Whittemore, Jones, and something."

They walked toward the gray-haired man who lay comfortably stretched on the ground with his head on a rolled-up jacket.

"Hi, Speed!" Chuck called. "Water cops give you a ticket?"

Leonard Whittemore stood up to greet them. Even in a tee-shirt he was a courtly man. "Andrea's really coming along, isn't she?" he said. And Andy felt her cheeks grow hot with more than wind burn.

One by one the other boats came in, Martha and Timmie trailing, a slow last. Timmie's head drooped almost onto his chest as he followed his mother up from the boat landing. But Andy saw the dead-white face, the clenched jaw. Without speaking to anyone he threw himself onto the ground face down.

In a second Andy was beside Martha. "What gives with Tim?"

A cluster of lines puckered between Martha's eyebrows. "No telling," she said. "Virus, seasickness, or maybe just temperament. Sometimes I think I'm all wrong to urge him into foldboating." For a moment Martha turned her face away. "Perhaps it's pure selfishness makes me do it. I see so little of the kid. He didn't really want to come today. Anyhow, his breakfast went overboard and he feels awful. I hope he snaps out of it before we have to start back."

"Poor little guy." Andy was thinking of Skeeter. How would Skeeter stand up to the ordeal of paddling across the bay when he could scarcely hold his head up? Then she began to feel amused. She knew her Skeeter. That stubborn little wretch would never have left home in the first place. Skeeter did what Skeeter wanted to do.

Long before the tide turned at 7 P.M. it became clear that Tim was not suffering an attack of temperament. Even without a thermometer it was plain that he was running a temperature.

Chuck came privately to Andy. "Whit has dug up a powerboat here in the cove willing to take Tim and Martha over to Sausalito—right now. From there they can catch a bus home. Martha's pretty worried." It was obvious that Chuck shared her feeling. "Whit says he will paddle Martha's big double back to Richmond if someone else will take his boat home. How about it?"

Andy gasped. "Me! Paddle through the dark alone! All by myself!"

"I'll stay close by. The ride home should be a breeze with the tide doing most of the work. Don't say yes, though, if it's going to make you jittery." Chuck stood with his hat in one hand, raking the hair on the top of

his head with the other. It was a familiar gesture and
always meant he was thinking hard.

"Of course I'll do it," Andy said. "Poor Timmie."

The ride home *was* a breeze. A stiff one. It came from
the wrong direction and swirled the bay into four-foot
swells and whitecaps. The tide was with the paddlers,
but the strong veering wind produced a current at right
angles to the tide, which made navigation difficult indeed. Andy tried to keep Chuck in sight and she knew
he was trying to keep her in sight, but in the dusk they
lost each other behind the swells. The advertised moon
was hidden behind a bank of fog which began rolling
in through the Golden Gate even before the sun went
down.

Andy was on her own now, in a strange boat, on a
rough black bay—alone with the pelicans and the bell
buoys. The paddling was hard, harder than anything
she had ever done. The darkness made everything
spooky. When a home-straggling pelican swooped
across the bow of her boat she was so startled she nearly
dropped the paddle. With all her heart she hoped
Mother would not look out the window of the living
room to see small white waves dotting the inky water.

This is my chance, Andrea told herself as she struggled to keep an even rhythm. My chance to prove what
I can do—to thank Chuck—to show him I'm really good.

Before she had gone halfway across the bay her
arms began to ache but she dared not rest. To stop
paddling even for a moment would let the boat swing
around, put it in danger of being swamped by the haystacks. No matter how her arms pained, she must keep
it headed straight into the waves. If she did upset, the
Mae West would of course keep her afloat, but it was
not likely that anyone would find her before morning.
The water of the bay was bitterly cold.

"Just a matter of brute strength," Chuck had said,

describing the trip. He didn't lie. That's for sure, Andy
thought as she dredged up all her reserves of strength
and will to keep going, to fight the throbbing of her
arms and shoulders and back.

Gong, gong, came the doleful warning of a bell buoy
on her left. She back-paddled furiously with her right
to avoid it. Stretch, pull, stretch, pull. Keep going. Try
to forget how much you hurt. Keep pushing ahead. She
tried singing to cut the eeriness of the dark, the night-
mare sensation that the entire world was filled with
heaving water, but every scrap of breath was needed
for paddling.

Long after time had ceased to exist, when she had
become an ice-cold automaton battling through black
water, praying she was headed in the right direction,
the lights of Point Richmond became visible on the horizon. They looked like magic lights to Andrea, more
wonderful than any Christmas tree out of her childhood. Even more beautiful than that tall and fragrant
fir beside which Don had once stood—what an eternity
ago that was—when he tossed her a little box containing a pair of silver skis.

At the thought of Don the rhythm of her paddling
faltered. Sternly she rebuked herself. Stop it. You dare
not think of Don now. That's over, buried, like the pin
at the very bottom of a pirate-painted toy chest under
a mountain of old ski clothes where no one will ever
find it. Only Andrea knew it was still there.

When at last she pulled ashore, Chuck and Whit were
standing on the beach circling flashlights for a signal,
their feet nearly in the water. They almost lifted her out
of the boat, beached it, and Chuck raised his flashlight
to peer into her face.

"You all right?" Andy nodded. "Had no idea I was
letting you in for a job like that—your first paddle alone.
I'm sorry, Andy. My fault. We should have left Martha's

boat at the cove and gone back for it another day. That wind blowing across the tide was sheer dynamite."

Andy tried to stretch her cramped arms, but they refused to move. "Everybody else in?" she panted.

"All except Connie. Go on up to the car. We'll wait here until he shows."

Half frozen, exhausted, Andy staggered away. Chuck came running after her. "Can you walk?" he demanded in a voice she scarcely knew.

"Of course I can walk." She wrenched her arm out of his grasp. No word of praise for getting safely into port, for keeping on course, for getting through with an unfamiliar boat. Guess that's just expected of you if you're a foldboater, Andy told herself as she dragged one foot after the other toward Whit's Cadillac. All in the night's work.

She threw herself down on the back seat, huddling into a coat someone had left there. Never in her life had she felt so tired. But it was a good tired.

CHAPTER FIVE

The gathering place for the boat trip down the canyon of Lodore was Vernal, Utah, a pretty little town of flat streets and green trees, near the northwest corner of Colorado. To reach Vernal from San Francisco required at least two days—long hard days of driving.

Chuck had offered to take both Andrea and Finette Reynolds in his car. Although Finette had not yet collected enough experience to attempt the Green River alone, Chuck felt that in the bow of his boat she would be safe. Also, her eagerness was hard to resist. Glad as she was to be piloting her own craft at last, Andy could not help a tweak of envy when she thought of Finette riding in the spot she had shared so long with Chuck. She would miss both his company and his judgment. Half of foldboating was deciding which way to jump.

After the river trip Chuck intended to drive on east to pick up a new car in Detroit. For the return to San Francisco his two passengers would be farmed out. Finette to the Monktons for a week of camping through Bryce and Zion National Parks; Andy to Martha Frayne. Tim would be with Martha, of course, as well as a foldboating nephew from Oregon.

Whit was flying both ways. Connie Van Fleet planned

to drive with his parents, who were not foldboaters but wished to see the river as passengers on the big rubber raft in which two professional boatmen would ferry duffle bags and provisions for the trip.

Andy had grown very fond of Finette since that cold winter day at the pool when Chuck first asked her to show the pretty girl from Minnesota how to hold a paddle. Although Andy was seventeen, Finette twenty-one, they never thought of each other as older and younger. In some ways Andy felt older than Finette. Finette seemed to have no problems, apparently never had had any. She was enthusiastic about her work at the store, liked everybody, and everybody liked her. She was the girl with the flute in the *Family of Man*, the girl with dancing eyes and lips set to a merry tune. She loved clothes, which were her business, and wore them well. But even dirty and disheveled after a day on the river, with hair mussed and lipstick gone, Finette managed a certain jauntiness. "Must be a touch of French in Finette's ancestry," Martha said.

During the long day of driving across Nevada, Chuck drew Finette on to talk about her work at the store. It was his way, his genius, Andy thought, to find out more about people than they knew about themselves.

"Right now I'm selling cotton dresses," Finette told him. "Fourteen ninety-eight stuff. But someday I'm going to be a buyer in suits or gowns—the French-room kind. I watch those old gals dishing out hundred- and two-hundred-dollar numbers like so much cheese. And every chance I get I pump them about what makes females tick when they buy clothes."

"What does?" Chuck inquired.

"Imagination is part of it. Women want to see themselves as more glamorous than they are. If you can make them feel that way—you're in. I'll learn," she added, full of her own special zest.

"I doubt you'll make that French room—in time——" Chuck told her dryly. Then abruptly he pressed down on the accelerator till his old Chevy hit seventy-five. "Getting so interested in Finette's career, I'm forgetting how many miles we have to cover today."

They zoomed on in silence for a time, smelling the sage, watching the sculptured clouds and cloud shadows turn the stark Nevada hills into a thousand shades from palest palomino to rich chocolate brown.

"How did those pioneer women ever have enough courage to cross Nevada?" Andy said wonderingly. "Imagine crawling through this desert with oxen—and little children. Not even knowing what was at the California end."

Chuck said, "Courage hasn't yet run out on this old planet."

"I think it took more than courage," Finette put in. "It took imagination. It's like what I said about women buying clothes. The people who endured across the deserts and mountains had a dream—a dream about themselves. About their life in California."

"I think you've got something there, Finette." Chuck tossed his cap onto the back seat, as if getting rid of a hatband would somehow free his brain for clearer thinking. "Imagination is what the people who wanted to dam up the Green River and flood Lodore and all the Yampa did *not* have. They couldn't get it through their skulls that people might need wilderness more than they need a little extra water and power." Andy thought she had never heard Chuck speak with so much fervor. "By cracky, it was one of the real thrills of my life when that bill to flood Dinosaur National Monument got batted down. It was the little voices that did it too. The little guys—thousands of 'em writing letters —with imagination that could see into the future."

"I wish I knew more about dinosaurs and all that ancient business," Finette said. "Every time I go to read about them I bog down in a lot of grim names. And as for those geological periods—I can't even pronounce, let alone remember those."

They laughed together at Finette's distress. Finette was that kind of a person. She could laugh at herself too.

"Lizard isn't a grim word to remember, is it, Finette?" Chuck asked.

"Of course not, but——"

"Well, dinosaur just means terrible lizard. That's what they were, too, those old reptiles. A few of them got up on their hind legs to grab off their food better. Sort of like kangaroos. But mostly they were just tremendous lizards with pint-size brains."

"Maybe that's why they didn't last," Andy suggested. "No imagination in their little heads."

"What exactly *is* a reptile?" Finette demanded.

"Well—if you want it in words of one syllable, it's a cold-blooded creature with a backbone, that lays eggs on land."

Finette's eyes twinkled. "They sound simply fascinating."

But Chuck was intent on the road and did not see her face.

"Fish live all their lives in the water. Amphibians developed next and they needed both land and water to keep going. After the amphibians (but before birds and mammals appeared on the earth) the reptiles came along and they made it the whole way on dry land. That was in the Mesozoic era."

"Ah-ah-ah!" Finette pointed an accusing finger at Chuck. "You promised words of one syllable."

"Okay. Call it middle time of life. Like that better?"

"Much better."

"The middle of geologic life was the dinosaur hey-day. About a hundred and forty million years ago. If you two gals don't heckle me too much we might get into Vernal early enough tonight to look in at the museum. It's full of dinosaur bones and paintings of dinosaurs and enough charts to keep you busy for a month. The best exhibit of dinosaurs, though, we'll see as we leave the river. There's another museum there where the main drift of skeletons was found."

In midafternoon the museum idea sounded fine. But by the time they reached Vernal, food and bed were the only important things in life. In the morning they had scant time to race through it before driving on to the home of Ollie Rawson, head boatman and king of all the river men.

Scrambled all over Ollie's lawn were bags of fold-boats, bags of clothing, fishing gear, cameras, sweaters, sun hats, jackets, and people. A yellow bus, which Fin-ette insisted had been used by the dinosaurs, was parked at the curb. Ollie, in overalls and a striped hick-ory shirt, was busy getting wooden boxes of food stowed inside the bus. He was being helped by a brawny youth who tossed fifty-pound parcels about like baseballs.

Before Andy and Finette could take in who had ar-rived and who had not, Martha Frayne walked quickly toward them, followed by her nephew.

"Greetings, children," she said gaily. "Have a good trip?" She didn't wait for an answer. It was written on both their faces. "This is my nephew, Lance Ferrier. He's the champion foldboater of the University of Ore-gon, and in case you two don't know it, Oregon is the place where they really have white water. Isn't that true, Lance?"

"True about the white water," Lance said. "There are not enough people at college interested in foldboating to have champion mean anything except that you have a boat and go out in it."

Andy looked at the gray-green eyes smiling confidently below a thatch of sandy hair. Almost angrily she thought, Why does this nephew have to be so smooth? Why couldn't he be shy and frightened like Timmie Frayne? Maybe then we could be friends.

Aloud she said, "Perhaps you'll teach us some new paddle tricks—Oregon style."

Lance shrugged. "Water's water, I guess, wherever you find it."

"What started you foldboating in the first place?" Finette asked him.

"My camera," Lance said. His easygoing expression became suddenly charged with interest. "My real passion is photographing wildlife—birds especially. And rivers take you into the wilderness faster and more easily than any other transportation."

Andy glanced at Finette's face. She was listening to Lance with a look of vivid interest. That's me all over, Andy thought. I make one remark to him and our conversation is finished. But first crack out of the box Finette has started him talking about *the* thing in the world that interests *him*.

Gently Finette prodded the talk. "What do you make? Movies, color, black and white?"

"For this trip I have two cameras with me, one movie and one still. I'm not sure it makes sense to carry both of them because when a picture breaks I usually manage to have the wrong camera. Birds don't like to wait around for the photographer."

The Monktons wheeled up to the curb just then with a screech of brakes and a flurry of flying gravel. Liz tumbled out, crying to all and sundry, "Dear heaven,

I thought I'd never get Monk out of that museum. I'm the wife who almost lost her husband to a darling lady Brontosaurus."

Martha grabbed her nephew by the hand and pulled him along. "Come on, Lance. You have two more people to meet and that's positively all."

"Well, I haven't met everybody yet," Andy said to Finette. "Those must be Connie's parents he's standing with, and isn't Connie a dead ringer for his mother?"

Finette eyed the tall lean woman as critically as if she were about to choose a dress for her. "Sort of like an overexposed color film, isn't she? Everything looks too pale to be real. I'm not sure whether she is blond, brunette, or mildly gray. And what's more, I don't think I care." Finette's gaze strayed to another part of the lawn. "But look! Over there. Talking his head off to Whit. Where did *he* materialize from?"

Andy wheeled to follow Finette's stare. A short stocky man, with hair Indian-black and Indian-straight above a classic profile, was leaning against a rubber dunnage bag, gesticulating vigorously as he talked. Strong even teeth showed very white against a skin darkened by years of exposure to sun and wind.

"Friend of Whit's, maybe?"

"Listen," Finette said sharply, cocking her head to one side like a small wise bird. "He has an accent. German, I think. Or possibly Austrian."

At that moment Ollie's outsize helper strode up behind the two men, swooped the rubber duffel bag up in his arms, and dumped the stranger sprawling on the grass like an overturned beetle. Quick as a cat, he was on his feet again, looking around to see who had upset him. A loud "haw-haw-haw" reverberated through the morning sunshine as the bag was pitched on top of the others in the rear of the bus.

"Not so funny," Andy said, watching the baggage

smasher with angry eyes. "No wonder Europeans think
all Americans are barbarians."

Her indignation was topped by the squawk of a
truck which came roaring out of Ollie's back yard to
pull up behind the bus.

"Here comes the big neoprene raft," Monk cried,
dragging Liz toward the truck. "Let's have a look at
her."

Andy followed them, but the heap of deflated rubber
on the floor of the truck had no resemblance that she
could see to any water-borne craft.

The bus ride was hot and tedious. In spite of the fact
that Ollie drove with breath-taking disregard for curves,
chuckholes, and human life, it seemed as if they
would never reach the "put in" place at Brown's Park.
After they left the paved highway a powdery dust rose
white and choking from the parched Colorado hills.
It seeped through closed windows, settling on hair,
slithering down collars, until Finette said even her
teeth felt dusty. They crossed the Yampa, running quietly between sandy banks, and lurched on northward
toward the point where Wyoming, Colorado, and
Utah come together.

At last Ollie called out, "Okay, Buzz. Get the gate."

Without bothering to use the steps Buzz jumped
from the bus and opened a cattle gate for Ollie to drive
through. "This is it, folks," he bellowed. "Welcome to
robbers' roost."

The bus creaked down a sandy bank, and under a
wide grove of sycamores Ollie jolted to a stop, slammed
on the brakes, and followed Buzz outside.

Now, at last, the excitement which had been so many
months building flared up again inside of Andrea. This
was it. The Green River, the big tributary to the Colorado, the river which should really have been named
Colorado. If you followed down the Green far enough

you could go all the way to Lake Mead and Hoover
Dam. If you had enough luck, that is, and enough skill
and strength. She was only going to travel a tiny piece
of the Green, from Brown's Park to Split Mountain. But
that little contained the canyon of Lodore.

Lunch was spread on a battered picnic table, but
Andy felt either too hot or too excited to eat. She drank
several cups of tomato juice and nibbled at a sandwich,
tossed most of it into the bushes for the squirrels. Then
hurried to pick out her two boat bags from the mound
of baggage piled beside the truck. How glad she was
now for all the practice hours she had spent in the living
room putting the boat together and taking it down
again. She could really do a smooth job.

Since leaving home Andrea had scarcely thought of
her family. Driving with Chuck, seeing a whole new
kind of country, talking to Finette at night in their
motel room had filled her world. It was fun talking to
Finette after the lights were out and they were both
in bed. Quite different from talking to Marianne. They
decided to go on spreading their sleeping bags side by
side for the rest of the trip.

But now, as the great moment approached, she suddenly wished her father were here, wished he could
know these people who were so big a part of her life.
How good it would be to see his broad tweed shoulders
standing beside Whit or Chuck under this leafy arch
of sycamores.

Most people were still eating lunch when Andy set
to work. This was the real thing at last—she was as-
sembling her own foldboat to put it in a real river. So
intent was she on studying the different pieces that she
was unaware of someone standing beside her, watching.
Her long, level eyebrows were caught in a pucker of
concentration as she examined each cross rib and longeron carefully to see which fitted where. Now and then

she pulled a bandanna from the pocket of her jeans
and mopped the perspiration that beaded her forehead.

The voice at her elbow startled her. She looked up
open-eyed to see Lance Ferrier peeling an orange as he
watched her fit the parts of the boat into place. "Like
an orange?" he asked. "You look hot."

"I am hot," Andy said, flopping back off her knees
to sit in the dust. "And I'd love an orange. Where did
you find them? I didn't see anything but tomato juice
laid out for lunch."

"Oh, I have a few stowed in my rucksack. But you'd
really be doing me a favor to eat one." He patted
the bulging bag slung over one shoulder.

"Film and filters and stuff?" Andy asked, remembering Finette's conversational gambit.

"And stuff is right." Lance handed her the peeled
orange and started another for himself.

"Aren't you afraid you'll upset someday and ruin
all that camera gear in the water?" Andy asked through
a mouthful of orange.

"There's always that chance, even with the best
waterproof covers. But I'll only keep one camera in my
own boat and just enough film for the day. The main
supply is going to travel in the raft with Ollie and Buzz
and that middle-aged couple."

"They're the Van Fleets. Connie's parents."

A quizzical twinkle came into Lance's face. "Oh—of
course. I sat near them in the bus but never did catch
up with their names. Mrs. Van Fleet is chatty as all
get out. Chiefly about Connie. Told me they had come
on this trip just to have a good visit with their son. They
stopped overnight in Reno especially so Connie could
see the gambling. 'We thought he ought to see that side
of life also,' Mama said. How old is this Connie, for
heaven's sake? I haven't picked him out yet."

Andy poked the last sections of orange into her

mouth and went back to work on the foldboat. "I don't
know exactly. He's in college."

"I take it you don't know him very well."

Andy looked up. "No. I suppose I don't. I don't believe any of us know Connie very well. He's an odd
fish."

"I can see why," Lance said, smiling in recollection.
Then abruptly his face tensed.

"Hey! Listen! I hear a motor chugging. I bet they're
inflating that raft thing." Lance grabbed Andy's hand
to pull her up from the ground. "Come on, let's go
watch." Moving with long rapid strides, he carried her
along so fast that Andy limped a little trying to keep
up with him.

"You're limping," Lance said, stopping short in his
tracks. "Did I jerk you up too hard? I'm terribly——"

"It's nothing," Andrea said, but her mouth grew fixed
and all the golden lights went out of her brown eyes.

Together they stood watching Buzz pump air into
the rim of the raft, but Andy could think of nothing
more to say. She yearned to get back to her boat, was
afraid it would seem rude to leave.

Lance was fascinated. "The thing's exactly like those
plastic wading pools people blow up for kids in the
back yard, isn't it? Except that it's black and oblong instead of round and yellow. What a monster it's going to
be!"

Andrea nodded. "I better go look after my boat," she
said brusquely. "Somebody might step on one of the
wooden pieces and break it."

"Want me to help you?" Lance asked.

"Oh no. No, thanks. I can set it up alone. Thanks
for the orange, though."

Slowly she walked back across the dusty flat of
Brown's Park. I'm still a cripple, she thought bitterly.
I'll never be able to dance and run and climb like other

girls. The square hands swinging at her sides clenched into fists. "I *will*, though. *Somehow* I will. I'll show them what I can do. I'll be the best woman foldboater in the world before I get through."

CHAPTER SIX

The afternoon sun was making heat waves dance over the surface of the river before all the food boxes and all the duffel bags were stacked in the center of the black neoprene raft, all the foldboats ready to leave.

Ollie sat down on a cross board in the stern of the raft, braced his feet on a plank, adjusted his suspenders, and picked up the oars. The small bright eyes in his weather-seamed face darted over the river, seeing every ripple, every pattern of wind, reading its meaning. Buzz, stripped to the waist, gripped the forward oars in his massive hands.

Clutching Mr. Van Fleet with one arm and Connie with the other, Mrs. Van Fleet stepped aboard. As her foot touched the flexible rubber floor she gave a piercing squeal. "Oh, Daddy! Help! The bottom of this thing is wiggly as a fish. You can feel the water bumping right through it. It'll never hold us."

Ollie smiled patiently and suggested she sit down.

"But where?" she asked. "Where is there to sit?"

"Just rest yourself on the baloney," Ollie told her, pointing to the inflated rim of the raft, wider than the back of a fat old horse. "No bumps for a long spell yet." He tossed her an end of rope fastened to the side of the raft. "Here. Hang onto this till you get used to riding."

Mrs. Van Fleet sat down, her feet dangling, held tensely to the rope with both thin white hands. Mr. Van Fleet eased himself down beside her. She kissed Connie good-by and Ollie pushed off.

As Mae Wests were being fastened and hats tied down against a gust of river wind, Chuck gathered his little company for a last word. "Today's run is just a shakedown cruise," he said, his face bright as a boy's with anticipation. "Only one stretch of fast water, and that's not too fast. If you get thirsty you can drink the river, but it won't taste like much."

Doesn't look like much either, Andy thought, eying the sluggish brown water, comparing it with the crystal streams of the Sierra Nevada.

"Tonight we camp at a place where there's a good cold spring. You can drink yourselves brimful after we land. You'd better too. No sense getting dehydrated in this hot sun. That only leads to a great waste of food." There were a few reminiscent titters in Chuck's audience. "You'll see the raft pulled up on the right-hand bank as a marker to stop. Kind of a sandy beach. Take it easy, everybody. Be seeing you." He grinned, steadied his boat for Finette to get in, and led off.

Immediately behind Chuck a narrow racing boat shot into midstream. The short dark man whom Andy had thought of as "the stranger" dipped his paddle lightly from side to side so that he seemed to flow through the water without effort.

"That's the most perfect paddling I ever looked at," Andy exclaimed to no one in particular.

"It ought to be. He's the German champion." She turned to find Lance Ferrier once more standing beside her. "Want a hand getting your boat down to the water? This mudbank is pretty steep."

Andy hesitated. The familiar words of little girlhood jumped first into her mind. "No. I do it mine ownself." But Lance Ferrier's face was so friendly, so outgoing, she found herself saying, "Thank you, yes. It will save scraping the bottom. How about your own boat?"

"I'll carry it over my head like a canoe. Thanks just the same."

Still fascinated watching the racing boat glide downstream, Andy made no move. "The river doesn't look as if it could ever be swift and menacing, does it?" she murmured. "Just a big old lazy puddle meant for fishing and lying in the sun."

"That's the fun of foldboating," Lance said. "You never know what lies around the corner."

Under the weight of the July sun all the boats paddled slowly. For Andrea the tense weeks of waiting, the sharp anticipation shot with worry dissolved into languor. Moving just fast enough to keep Chuck's straw hat in sight, she had again the swan sensation she had felt on the Russian River the first day Monk put a double-bladed paddle in her hand. But this time the smoothness of the ride was her own doing.

Whit passed her, then Liz and Monk. She didn't care at all. For once her urge to compete was dozing. Today she was part of the river, part of the sun, the poplar trees, and willows drooping on the banks. Drowsy warmth penetrated to her very marrow. Swallows were skimming the surface of the water in graceful arcs and she saw Lance floating in a back eddy against the bank, trying to photograph them. What a lot of trouble, Andy thought—this picture taking. The rhythm of the paddle was almost narcotic.

Then abruptly the river narrowed, the muddy banks ended, and dark red cliffs shot with purple shadows rose a thousand feet above the water. Involuntarily Andrea sucked in her breath and braced her knees more

firmly under the canvas deck. Here it was at last—the
gateway to Lodore.

> "Here it comes sparkling,
> And there it lies darkling,
> Now smoking and frothing
> It's tumult and wrath in."

Old Southey never saw anything like this in mild little
England, she told herself. Her paddle dug the water
faster in time to the lilt of the poem as the tiny boat slid
into the shadow of the cliffs. No sandy channel here.
Water sluiced straight through stone where a mountain
range had been pierced by a river. In an instant the
languor of lazy water and hot sun dropped away, re-
placed by a feeling of awe. No wonder the Indians
peopled this canyon with jealous spirits. Who wouldn't
be jealous of cliffs like these?

She leaned forward to listen. There it was. The unmistakable roar. Muffled, dim, but coming closer. The
crash of swift water, terror, and delight. Louder and
louder it came, echoing between the bold rock walls
until it was thunder in her ears.

She stroked faster to keep Chuck in sight, to see how
he planned to take this rapid. He had pulled in close to
the right-hand bank where the river had undercut the
stone wall. The power of water to wear down rock was
unbelievable. Andy followed. The current swept him
diagonally across the river; he back-paddled hard on
the left to slow his speed and in another moment there
he was—sailing through quiet water again. Andy took
it precisely the same way and felt a quiver of triumph.
Not because it was difficult. She had gone through
harder rapids than these. But because it was Lodore
and she was on her own.

After dinner, in the long summer twilight, everyone

gathered around a driftwood fire at the edge of the river. Here Chuck officially introduced the newcomers, Lance Ferrier, Ollie and Buzz, the German champion, and urged each one to say a word or two about himself.

"This is Johan Speiser," Chuck told them, "who came to America last month to compete in the annual foldboat race on the Arkansas. We're pretty proud to have him join the River Runners for this shoot through Lodore. Tell us about the race, Johan, won't you? I don't think anyone here has ever been to one."

Johan stood up, thrust his hands into his pockets, and looked around at the firelit faces. "Well," he said with a wry half-smile, "the main thing is that after I get here I am not allowed to compete. Sometimes in Germany I give lessons in foldboat technique for money which I need. So in America I am not any longer amateur. This is very sad for me. But your officials did the best they could. They ask me to pace the race. Even though I cannot win, still it is a fine ride. Is a magnificent river, that Arkansas in the middle of June. Twenty-six miles we go, from Salida to Cotopaxi, all dressed up in our crash helmets. I am lucky to get through without any swimming."

"How long did it take you?" Monk wanted to know.

"Two hours, forty-six minutes. My arms are quite strong." He doubled up an elbow so that the muscles bulged through his shirt. "Still I am very tired when I finish. I am—how you call it? Pooped."

There was laughter as he sat down again. It did not seem possible that the sturdy young man they had seen paddling the narrow slalom boat with such easy grace could ever feel weary.

Buzz next lumbered to his feet. In the tricky half-light he looked twice as tall as Johan Speiser. "Football's my racket," he drawled. "University of Utah. When I graduate, or maybe it'll be quituate, I expect to take up

one of my pro offers. Great game, football, and pro
football's the best. Meantime rowing rapids for Ollie in
summer keeps my wind good and my shoulder muscles
in shape." In unconscious imitation of Johan's gesture
he doubled up one arm. "Guess that's all about me except I play the harmonica." He whipped one out of a
shirt pocket, cupped his hands, and blew a rippling
blast before sprawling again on the sand.

Finette, sitting next to Andy on an old log, whispered,
"Shy little number, isn't he?" and they both giggled
softly together.

"Let's hear from Lance Ferrier now," Chuck said.
"We can really claim Lance as part of the River Runner family because he is Martha's nephew. Still, just
for the record, we'd like to have a few facts about him."

Before he said anything Lance let his eyes travel all
the way around the circle of faces. They were alert,
friendly eyes and seemed to pull everyone there into
the circle of his friendship. His voice was low and relaxed
but quite easy to hear.

"There's not much to tell about me. Next year I'll be
a junior at the University of Oregon and I like foldboating. The other thing I get excited about is taking pictures of wild birds. I'm hoping to get some good shots
of Canadian geese on this trip and, if I'm lucky, a
golden eagle. If any of you spot an eagle soaring around
these cliffs I hope you'll drag me out of bed or even
away from my dinner to look. That about wraps it up,
I think, except that I'm awfully glad Tim is my cousin
and Martha is my aunt."

Again Finette leaned close to Andy's ear. "There's a
really nice guy. If he were a few years older I'd give
you a run for your money, Andy."

"Don't be silly," Andy whispered back. "Lance won't
be interested in me. Boys aren't. He's just nice to everybody that comes along."

Finette started to argue this, but Andy put a finger on her lips. "Sh-sh," she hissed as Chuck said, "Now here's the man who has forgotten more about the Green River than any of us will ever know."

Ollie did not stand when he was introduced. He shoved his cap to a more precarious angle on the back of his head, tossed away the straw he was sucking, and, leaning comfortably on one elbow, said, "I'm Ollie Rawson—river rat. This morning I put into the water ahead of the rest of you, but when we come to the big rapids Buzz and I will bring up the rear so we can pick up the guys that take a ducking." Ollie made a grunting noise somewhere in the back of his throat. "I wouldn't go down this river in one of those little bugs you ride for fame *or* money. Let alone fun."

He looked up at the darkening sky and thought a minute before he went on. "Nothing very interesting about me. I been around this dinosaur country a long while. Guess you can tell that by looking at me. But maybe some of the yarns I've picked up over the years might keep you awake.

"That Brown's Park we started at today is kind of a famous place. Remember Buzz here saying, 'Welcome to robbers' roost' when he opened the gate for the bus? That's what folks used to call Brown's Park. It's so close to the corner where Colorado, Utah, and Wyoming come together that cattle rustlers used to like to hide out there. If the law from one state came after them they'd beat it over the line and laugh at the sheriff. Fella named Butch Cassidy was the most famous of that gang. Kind of a modern Robin Hood he was. All the ranchers around Brown's Park protected him because he was mighty good to them. Even rode into town one hard winter when the ranch people was flat broke and brought grub back to them, in spite of there being

a reward out for Butch, dead or alive, for train rob-
bery."

"Look at Timmie," Andy said under her breath. "His
eyes are bugging right out of his head." It was true.
Tim was listening to Ollie as if his life depended on
remembering every word.

"Some folks say this Butch Cassidy got away to
Mexico finally, then slipped back into the U.S. after a
few years, and that he's still living here under another
name. Living like a God-fearing citizen."

Timmie could stand it no longer. "Do you think that's
true, Ollie? About Butch, I mean."

Ollie rubbed his chin with a horny palm. "Couldn't
say, fella. I'm just telling you the story the way I heard
it."

"But why is it called Brown's Park instead of Butch
Cassidy's Park?" Timmie demanded.

"Oh, that's another yarn entirely. Baptiste Brown
lived there years ahead of Cassidy. He was a French
Canadian trapper. You see, this park is the most protected place anywheres around in winter. Always grass
for horses and cattle there, which the Indians knew
better'n anybody. So naturally the Indians didn't care
much about having the trappers run 'em out of it."

Ollie sounded as if he were about to stop talking,
but Timmie kept prodding him.

"Well, this Brown was making the rounds of his
beaver traps one day when he heard war cries. So right
away he knew the Blackfeet were on the warpath. He
dug his spurs into his horse and rode to where he knew
there was a narrow gorge in the river. The Indians were
right behind him when he jumped his horse across that
gorge. The horse was killed and Brown broke both his
legs falling on the rocks, but the Indians couldn't get
to him. Couple of days later some other trappers following the trail of his horse rescued him. They set the

bones in his legs and for two months they hauled him around in a litter strung between two pack animals. No wonder every time Indians was mentioned Baptiste used to yell, 'Keel 'em all.' Well—I could go on all night telling you stories. But I'm not agoin' to."

There were cries of "Go on, Ollie. Don't stop yet."

But the boatman shook his head. "I might get started on my favorite character, Queen Ann Bassett, and then you never would get to hit the sack."

"Why is she your favorite, Ollie?" Liz asked.

"I guess because she had so much spunk. Roped a grizzly cub when she was thirteen and nigh got clawed to death by the mother bear doing it. Rode and handled a gun like a cowboy, and when her family sent her off to board at a convent finally for the nuns to make a lady of her she sure wrecked the place." Ollie chortled in appreciation of Ann Bassett's spirit. "That's all tonight now. Chuck wants to talk to you about tomorrow's run through Disaster Falls. It's all yours, Chuck." Ollie picked another twig and resumed his chewing.

"Are they really falls?" Timmie wanted to know. His excitement over Ollie's history had turned to tenseness.

"Naw, they're just rapids," Ollie told him. "Two of 'em. Upper and Lower Disaster. Powell named them that because he lost one of his boats there. But Powell didn't know much about running in white water and his boats were no good for it anyhow."

Chuck took over the campfire then, briefing them on what to expect on the river, as well as giving a few statistics about hours of eating and leaving and who was elected to K.P.

When he had finished, Buzz took out his harmonica and began to play softly. A few people changed seats, to be warmer or cooler, or to hunt for the smokeless side of the fire.

"Come on, everybody, sing," Buzz ordered. Leonard

Whittemore's powerful baritone rang out with "Home,
Home on the Range" and the rest followed.

Singing lustily, Lance drifted across the circle toward Andrea and Finette. "Come on and sing, Andy.
You must know the words to this one."

"I know the words all right," Andy said, "but I'd better not sing." She wanted to sing because it was a way
of shouting politely about how happy you felt.

"Aw, come on, Andy. I'm no opera star either, but
it's fun to sing."

She shook her head. "I can't stay on the tune," she
said woefully. "Even my family won't let me sing outside of a shower." Lance must like her a little or he
wouldn't have made the special effort to sit by her. She
wasn't going to ruin that by letting him laugh at her
off-key performance.

After a few more songs campfire broke up. Timmie
said good night to his mother and went off proudly with
Lance to camp at the boys' end of the flat.

Martha, Finette, and Andy picked their way toward
the clump of Utah juniper behind which their sleeping
bags were spread. Each one held a flashlight and they
stepped carefully to avoid the clumps of cactus which
could easily penetrate a canvas tennis shoe.

Settled inside her bag at last, Martha Frayne heaved
a big sigh. "I do hope Tim hasn't put his air mattress
down on this prickly pear," she said to the other two.

"Of course he won't," Finette said cheerily. "Why,
Tim's a scout."

"I know," Martha murmured, as much to herself as to
the girls. "But Tim's a scout the hard way. He never
would have stuck the out-of-door part of it if a cagey
scoutmaster hadn't thought to make him scribe for the
troop. I don't believe they ever had a scribe before, but
Tim's it. And getting out that one-page mimeographed

newspaper every week is the most vital thing in his life."

Andrea closed her eyes and let her whole body sink limply against the cushion of air. "Lance will take care of him, Martha. I'm sure he will," she said drowsily. And in her mind she kept seeing a head of unruly hair above a pair of friendly eyes that smiled directly into hers.

CHAPTER SEVEN

The next morning Andy was dressed and packed before Whit and Martha had breakfast ready. As quickly as she could thread between the juniper and cactus, she went down to make sure her boat was still secure. She knew, of course, that it was. It had been pulled well up onto the beach and there had been no flash flood to make the water rise during the night. Nevertheless, she wanted to see it, touch it, smooth it with her fingers, to experience all over again the delicious feeling that it was really hers.

The slender beauty was still there, lined up with seven others and the clumsy black raft. She examined the paddle. It still had two blades. The white float balls were dangling over the edge just as she had left them; the bottle of Sea and Ski lay on the floor. Closing her eyes, she felt herself again inside the boat, flying at delirious speed down the high-walled canyon of Lodore.

When she opened them again to take a good look at the morning she noticed Timmie Frayne sitting alone at the other end of the beach. His knees were drawn up, clasped within his arms, his head tilted back as he stared at the cliffs across the river. Picking her way over the debris of water-bleached wood and brush, Andy sat down beside him. The boy's thin face was pinched with worry.

"What's up, Tim?" she asked softly.

He answered without taking his eyes from the cliffs. "I shouldn't have come."

"But why? Aren't you having fun? You loved Ollie's stories last night."

"Oh, Andy, I'm scared. I guess that's what it is. Don't tell anybody I said so, though." He laid his forehead on his knees, embarrassed at having exposed so much of himself.

"Of course I won't tell, Tim. But why are you scared? You're a good paddler. And your mother has been a River Runner for years. She's superb."

"I know she is. That's the main reason I came. She wanted me to so much. But when my mother calls out, 'Paddle hard left,' or 'Back-paddle right. Harder, Timmie, faster,' all I see is those cliffs and the water rushing around like a crazy bull and—I don't know why it is—I get mixed up or something and do the wrong thing." He looked up at Andy with deep-set intelligent eyes, full of bewilderment. "Mother gets such a boot out of foldboating herself she can't understand why I'd rather stay home and read." Once started, the bottled-up words came pouring out of Tim in a torrent. "Of course I know you can't read all the time. You have to do things too. I don't wish to become a recluse."

Andy wanted to laugh at Tim's pompous phrase. At the same time it brought a lump into her throat. Tim was suffering. Martha must know it and was probably suffering even more. Getting Lance to come with the River Runners had been partly to help Tim, though Martha was fond of Lance for his own sake. How could she help it? Andy thought.

"Lance is such a normal, happy person, I know he'll be good for Tim," Martha had said. "A thirteen-year-old needs a father," she added in one of those rare moments when she spoke of her own problems. "A big brother is next best."

"Listen, Tim," Andy began finally. "I don't know whether this will help you at all. It's something my father said to me once when I'd been teasing my brother because he was chicken about skiing. Skeeter is just about your age. He'll be thirteen next month. 'Let the kid alone,' Dad told me. Dad was stern when he said it, too. 'He has as much right to be scared as you have not to be. Sometimes frightened people are just people with more imagination than others. They visualize the things which might happen.' Then Dad laughed in a special down-in-the-throat way he has and said, 'You know, Andy, I hate to criticize the Lord's handiwork, but when he stirred up the batter for you he left out one awfully useful ingredient—fear.' Dad meant that the way I went tearing downhill on skis was crazy."

"Is that how you wrecked your knee, Andy? Being crazy?"

"No, it wasn't. The accident was not my fault. But what I'm trying to say is that maybe you have more imagination about foldboating than the rest of us. Maybe it's the rest of us who are crazy. Lots of people think so."

"Lance isn't crazy. He really thinks. About all sorts of things. You should hear the things he talks about when we're going to bed. And besides that, he's brave and he has imagination. One of his bird pictures even took some kind of a prize."

"But you're *you*, Timmie. And there's no sense your trying to be Lance."

Tim sighed mightily. "I wish I were. And I bet my mother wishes so too."

The sound of a tin plate being hammered with a spoon cut short any answer Andy might have made.

They both started back for breakfast as fast as they could go.

"Did you know Chuck drew my name out of the hat for K.P. tonight?" Tim asked as they scuttled toward the cooking fire. "And guess who I get to work with."

"This early in the game it could be anybody."

"Well, it's Mrs. Van Fleet," Tim said, making a face. "And something tells me you better eat all you can hold this morning."

Lance arrived at breakfast in high excitement. "I got some wonderful shots of Canada geese," he announced. "At least I hope they're wonderful. Right after daylight I heard a gentle kind of honking and bolted out of my sleeping bag, telling myself what a dope I was to crawl out that early when it would only turn out to be another wedge of geese flying in the stratosphere. I followed the sound for a while and finally found them only a few hundred yards upstream. They were feeding in a patch of sedgy stuff. I had to wade almost up to my waist to get close enough, and every minute I thought they'd take off. Canada geese are wary critters. But the wind must have been in my favor, or else they were as hungry as I am now, because they didn't stir. Just went on eating and talking—a pair of them and five goslings. Boy oh boy! It was the chance of a lifetime." All at once Lance came back to earth. "Hope you cooked great quantities of breakfast, Aunt Martha, because I could eat a raw grizzly bear."

"Come and get it," Martha said. "If it isn't enough, I'll scramble another pan of eggs just for you."

"You're as bad as the Dawson family, Lance," Andy told him, looking up from a well-heaped plate. "I always thought nobody—but nobody—could go as loco over his pet project as a Dawson."

"This was a rare chance, Andy. I only hope my exposures are right. They have such *beau*-tiful heads, those

Canada geese." He drew the word out as he pictured them. "Jet black with a broad white chin strap, set on long black necks."

"Just a gone goose is what you are," Andy told him, smiling.

Lance wrinkled his nose at her and got up to refill his plate.

Yesterday's shakedown cruise had successfully done the shaking. This morning there were no boats to set up. The baggage lay in a heap on the beach, and as soon as the food boxes were stowed Buzz tossed the duffel bags on top of them as if they had been so many sofa pillows.

Mrs. Van Fleet, curiously pale among so many brown faces stood beside the raft waiting for Ollie. Fearful lest it drift away, she refused to put foot inside the monster until Ollie was at the oars.

"That Buzz is the strongest person I ever saw," she said to Andy, who was tying on her Mae West. "I wish my Connie had a fraction of his muscle. Poor Connie, he just can't seem to put on an ounce of flesh."

Poor Connie—period, Andy said to herself, thinking back to Lance's remark. Perhaps this pale, timid woman really was the answer to Connie's differentness. Did parents actually have that much effect on their children?

The mother's voice carried on: "And I don't suppose Buzz ever gets tired."

"That's why I hired him," Ollie said, coming up in time to hear the last remark. "I'm getting too old to buck baggage. But Buzz ought to be husky. They say he's the best tackle Utah ever had. Keeps in training all year round, and when he isn't playing football he's throwing basketballs. Buzz would rather be named All-American tackle than go to heaven. Wouldn't you, kid?"

Andrea did not wait to hear Buzz's answer. She
stepped into her own boat and moved out where she
could be alone with the river.

Again she looked up at the canyon walls. Every hour,
as the light changed, they took on a different character.
Sometimes they seemed soft and rosy, protective; again
they turned to a strange purple, gloomy and menacing.
Each bend in the river revealed new shades of color in
this great gorge. And to think they might have dammed
it up, made it into just another mud-rimmed artificial
lake. Her eyes lingered over the rock ledges where juniper rooted in a fistful of humus, lifted higher to the
pines and firs. She knew they were pines and firs only
because Lance, looking through binoculars, had told
her so. The water was calm now; she could afford to
look up. Presently the ripples would start and all her
mind would be concentrated on watching the current,
on detecting hidden rocks by a telltale wave.

There was enough flow to carry her along without
much effort and, sitting low on the bottom of the boat,
she felt truly a part of the river. She belonged to it, as
a fish belongs.

Then far off she caught the deep-throated rumble of
white water. It was a challenge that sent blood racing
through her veins. But in Andrea there was no fear at
all, only excitement at the thought of overcoming this
powerful antagonist—the river.

Poor Timmie, she thought. All this and he doesn't
really like it. Tim seemed younger than Skeeter somehow. There was a tough core at the center of Skeeter's
being which would always protect him. Perhaps, Andy
speculated, this hero worship of Lance will help Tim
over the hump. No room in her mind now for Timmie,
though. No room for anything except how best to maneuver the boat. Paddle left, back-paddle right, watch
out for that snag. What's under this patch of foam? To

look away from white water even for a second was to
flirt with tragedy.

Chuck and Johan passed her, paddling side by side.
Finette, in the bow of Chuck's boat, looked more tense
than Andy had ever seen her.

"This is it," Chuck shouted above the roar of the water. "Upper Disaster coming up."

The river was narrowing, the current growing swifter.
Paddling now was not to propel the boat forward, but
to hold it back. Every second she picked up more speed.
It was like skiing again—the whish of her body against
the air, the delicate balance, split-second decisions, the
joy of keeping under control, of missing catastrophe by
inches.

She saw a wave break over Johan's boat. Chuck and
Finette followed him into the spray, and Andrea shot
into the channel after them. The bow of the boat went
down, water foamed over the deck, drenched her whole
head. No time to recover before another wave faced her.
But she was still right side up. Chuck had said she
could do it, and now she was doing it.

"Oh frabjous day, kaloo, kalay," she sang into the tu-
mult of the Green, which was louder and more satisfy-
ing to sing to than any bath water in the world.

The river did not become smooth between Upper
and Lower Disaster. Not millpond quiet, that is, the
way it had been back at Brown's Park. Was it only
yesterday they had eaten lunch under the sycamores?
Only yesterday she had been introduced to Lance and
thought, Why couldn't he be an odd fish who might
like another odd fish? Already she seemed to know him
better than she knew Connie Van Fleet after two years.
Connie was a character and no mistake. Now she was
glad that Lance was neither odd nor shy.

These ideas did not come all at once. They fluttered
in and out between the all-absorbing business of pad-

dling. That was the wonderful part of foldboating. Your
mind was swept up in it. You couldn't stop to be sorry
for yourself because you were not able to walk as far
or dance as well as other girls. If you did, that would
be the finish of foldboating and of you too.

Lower Disaster was reported to be tougher than
Upper. Still keeping Johan and Chuck in sight, Andy
tried again to pick the route they were taking, but in
the end she had to depend on herself and nobody else.
In the foam of tearing water it was impossible to keep
close to anyone. It was every man for himself.

Two years of foldboating had strengthened her arms
as skiing had once strengthened her legs and knees.
She would need strong arms to win the big race someday. And if she was going to be a foldboater at all,
she was going to win. The Arkansas race was the pin-
nacle, the top—the All-American team, Buzz would have
called it. Two hours and forty-six minutes, Johan had
said it took him to make the run. That was a grueling
length of time to fight against rapids. She must remember to ask him what the best time was for a woman on
that wild and turbulent course.

She saw Chuck take off his hat and wave it in the
air. We're there, she thought. This must be Lower Disaster, where Powell left his boat upside down on the
rocks. The hat was to catch attention, but when both
Chuck and Finette gestured with their left arms she
was not sure whether they meant go to the left or stay
away from the left. Evidently they meant stay away because they were veering right, hugging the right wall of
the river. When she came up to the place where they
had waved she understood.

There was a slick of water on the left which looked
easy but probably concealed a rock. On the right the
river funneled between two enormous boulders. To
strike either one could be fatal, swinging the boat

around at right angles to the current. The pressure
of this river against the side of a boat plastered against
an immovable object amounted to thousands of pounds.
It would crush the fragile ribs like an egg shell.

This job was going to take all her strength and all
her skill. Left to herself, she would certainly have chosen the left-hand side of the river. But Andy had infinite faith in Chuck. Over and over she had seen his
judgment vindicated in those instantaneous decisions
she had watched him make on the Merced, the Stanislaus, and the Feather in California. This was more furi-
ous water than she had ever seen before, but she was
still ready to follow the little man in the straw hat.

Like a giant hand, the current seized the boat, rushed
it into the flume between the rocks. There was a
mighty whoosh of water. Andy leaned as far back as
she was able, saw a blue bow rise through the foam.
She bent forward again to help the boat recover and
seconds later floated into a quiet cove.

On the rocky bank of the cove Johan, Finette, and
Chuck were pulling their boats out of the water. Evidently they had chosen this easy landing place for
lunch. She was just curving toward them when she
heard a cry behind her back. Tim's voice! A boat was
upside down, two heads bobbed in the water. Martha
had chosen the left-hand side, which looked so smooth
and easy. Now she was struggling to reach her capsized
boat but making little progress. She still held a paddle
in her hand, but the other paddle was catapulting
along through the rapids. Tim, meanwhile was swimming away from the overturned boat toward shore.

"Oh, Timmie darling," Andrea said aloud, "you're
scared. And after this you'll be even more scared. Why
didn't you stick with the boat?"

It was impossible to paddle upstream to help Martha.
Anyhow, Chuck and Johan had seen the spill and were

both far better able to help than she was. The thing to
do was to go after Tim's paddle.

She turned the bow of the boat toward the outlet of
the cove and dipped hard. If she could get below the
paddle before it entered the next swift water she might
be able to catch it. There were, of course, extra paddles
in the raft. Nevertheless, to lose one was unfortunate,
particularly for Martha, who had to count all the pen-
nies. Worst of all, it would embarrass Tim, who was already jittery.

Andy took one more look to see what was happen-
ing. Martha had reached her boat finally and was
clinging to one of the float balls dangling over the stern.
Only then did it dawn on Andy that chasing Tim's
paddle was needless. A strong back eddy in the cove
was already carrying it in a half circle so that it would
lodge against the bank.

Johan meanwhile had clambered over the rocks to a
point where Martha could hear his voice. Through
cupped hands he was giving her some sort of advice.
Then Andy saw Martha deliberately let go of the boat,
which coasted down into the cove and followed the
curve of the paddle toward shore. Martha began swimming to Tim, who sat dripping on a rock. When the
empty boat came close enough Chuck waded out to pull
it in.

One by one the other boats came safely down the
river, the raft last of all.

"What happened, Martha?" Chuck asked. "Did you
hit a rock? Your boat looks all right. We turned it over
and couldn't see any marks on the bottom."

Martha spread her hands in a gesture which meant
"Who knows?"

But Tim spoke up quickly. "It was my fault," he
said. "When I saw a big old snag under the water I
got excited and leaned the wrong way. The next min-

ute we were both in the water. Mother said, 'Go after
your paddle. I'll hold the boat.' So I started. But it
was too far ahead of me to catch, so I just made for
dry land. Boy! Am I glad the boat's not wrecked! I
ought to be made to walk the rest of the way." Tim's
voice cracked a little as he moved away from the group
huddled about Martha's boat and stood by himself
looking intently at the mountain peaks, purple-black
against a bright blue sky.

"Poor kid," Andy said.

Chuck looked at the boy's back where the shoulder
blades were clearly outlined under his wet shirt. "He's
taking it hard."

"It's Tim's way to take things hard," Martha said,
and her face, usually so serene, was full of compassion.

Monk brought a billy can from his boat while Liz
gathered sticks for a small tea fire. Ollie produced a
large can of powered orange crystals and walked
around shaking them into each outstretched cup.

"May not be as good as that stuff they call fresh
frozen, but it sure makes this old river taste better," he
told them with pride. Ollie himself gulped three cupfuls
in quick succession. "Rowin' in the sun all day reely
takes the juice out of a man. Got to put it back in—some
way."

When the lunch bags were passed out Tim came
back to get his and sat down on the ground next to
Andy. He took a piece of cheese out of the bag, then
held it in his hand, just looking at it.

Buzz, sprawled on the other side of Andy, watched
him. "Don't you like our Utah cheese, kid? You better
eat it. It'll put meat on your bones."

Without answering, Tim dropped the cheese back
into the bag.

Buzz laughed. "Lost your appetite, huh? You
shouldn't let a little ducking scare you that much."

Flaring into sudden anger against this stolid man at
her side, Andy sputtered, "Leave the boy alone."

Still smiling, Buzz looked her up and down with an
appreciative eye. "Gosh, you look pretty when you get
mad. That cute little chin of yours sticks out like a
prize fighter. I'll have to figure out some way to keep
you mad all the time."

"If Tim doesn't want to eat that's *his* business,"
Andy snapped back. "Not yours."

"Some spitfire! I sure like a gal with spirit. Gives a
man a real challenge." Still grinning, Buzz rubbed his
hands together.

"Let's talk about something else," Andy said. "Not
about Tim and not about me. Did you row for Ollie
last summer too?" That was Finette's way, she thought.
Make him talk about himself.

"Last summer I'd never even heard of Ollie. I got
my workout bucking baggage for a hotel in Grand Canyon, up on the north rim. Pretty nice setup there too.
College girls waiting on table and college boys doing
other kinds of jobs. We all had a swell time together,
but this river job is better conditioning for football."

"And that's what you want most of all in the summer, isn't it?"

"That's what a fella has to have if he's going to cut
the buck at football. I got talked about for All-American last year but didn't quite make the grade. This year
is my last chance."

"Do you care terribly about being All-American,
Buzz?"

"Care! Well, for crying out loud!" The punch Buzz
put behind his words gave Andy a quick insight into
the drive which propelled this big body. "Of course I
care. All-American is the best you can be in football.
I want to get to the top."

Finette's system is certainly working, Andy thought.

I seem to have really unleashed something. Aloud she said, "I know how you feel. That's the way I feel about foldboating. Someday I want to get into the Salida race—and win——"she added truthfully.

She looked again at Buzz and her anger against him dissolved.

That evening Buzz made a plain and deliberate point of sitting next to Andy at campfire. He sat very close to her. She tried to edge away but there was not much space to edge into without moving onto Mr. Van Fleet's lap. Anyhow, she didn't want to be too obvious about the thing. Buzz was such a big hulking guy, he probably didn't realize how he was crowding her.

Later in the evening she found that sitting close had not been accidental. As campfire broke up, Buzz grasped her arm and turned her around to face the river. "Look," he said. "The moon." It had risen above the canyon wall and was now sending shafts of light dancing over the water.

"Ooh, lovely!" Andy said appreciatively.

"Come on, let's have a better look at it where the trees don't get in our way." Almost forcibly he propelled her away from the fire and down the bank to the beach where the boats were lined up waiting for a new day.

The minute she started toward the beach Andy realized she didn't in the least want to go moon-viewing with Buzz. She had a pretty clear inkling of what was coming, but couldn't think fast enough to get herself out of it. Every excuse that came to her mind sounded silly or stuffy. Afterward she realized that she might have called back to Finette or Martha to come join them. But Buzz rushed her along too fast to think.

Just beyond the line-up of boats the beach made a slight curve, and before Andrea could protest they were around the bend, with a thick clump of willow between them and the campfire.

Buzz wasted no time. In one practiced gesture he slid both arms around Andrea, held her firmly against his body, and kissed her so hard that she thought her neck was going to break.

Angrily Andy beat on his chest with both imprisoned fists. This was no friendly kiss. It was frightening.

"Let me go," she cried furiously when his mouth lifted from hers for a moment. "Take your hands off me."

But Buzz still held her in a vise. "Been wanting to do this ever since you got mad at me today. Golly, you looked pretty there, sticking up for that sissy boy."

"He's not a sissy," Andy retorted, forgetting herself for a moment. "He just has more imagination than certain other people I could mention."

"That's a hot one." Buzz laughed uproariously and, in so doing, relaxed his hold.

Andy flung out of his arms, stood facing him, shivering with rage.

"You don't expect to make me jealous of that pup, do you?" Buzz chortled.

"I don't expect anything, or want anything, except that you should never touch me again. Don't come near me!"

"Holy Toledo! What kind of a gal are you? Human?"

Andy stormed on, "I don't know what kind of a girl I am. But I'm sure I don't want to be pawed by you. I don't go in for necking. And if I did, it wouldn't be with you."

"Hey, calm yourself, sister. I haven't done anything so terrible. And don't call it necking. Up in Grand Canyon they've got a much more beautiful word. There, when you take a girl out to see the view it's called rimming."

Buzz's beautiful word was lost on Andy. She was scrambling back toward the campfire as fast as she could go.

Several people were still standing about, reluctant as always to pull themselves away from the glowing embers. Andy moved into the group and stood close beside Finette.

"What did you do with Buzz?" Finette whispered. "Not ten minutes ago I saw the two of you barging down to the river."

"I drowned him," Andy muttered between her teeth. "He had it coming."

Finette threw back her head and laughed—her special rippling laugh—which took some of the sting out of the situation for Andy. "I was afraid of something like that," she murmured. "Live and learn, baby." Fondly she slipped an arm around Andrea's waist and they wandered off together to find their sleeping bags.

"Did Lance see me take off with Buzz?" Andy asked, glancing over her shoulder to see whether they were alone.

There was a perceptible pause before Finette answered. "I'm not sure. He talked to me for a minute as campfire broke up, but I'm pretty sure it was you he was looking for."

"Lance will probably never speak to me again," Andy murmured.

"Oh, I wouldn't say that. Buzz might whet his interest."

"I feel like a fool," Andy said. "And I don't like the feeling one bit."

Their voices dropped to nothing when they found Martha already asleep. "Poor Martha," Finette said. "She had a tough day."

Andy rummaged for a hairbrush in her duffel bag, leaned back against a rock, brushing in jerks. Finette sat cross-legged on top of her bed, deftly turning her own hair into waves. Through a mouthful of bobby pins she mumbled, "In this moonlight your hair looks exactly like taffy candy. Good enough to eat."

"Hair like taffy but the girl was daffy," Andy whispered back. "I'm afraid you're full of delusions about me."

Poking the last bobby pin into place, Finette walked over to Andy and shook her by the shoulders. "For heaven's sake, stop worrying, will you? Buzz is only one of a whole pack of wolves wandering around the world. And he doesn't even wear sheep's clothing."

CHAPTER EIGHT

Andrea slept fitfully that night. The moon glittered too brightly in her eyes, and when to escape it she buried her head inside the sleeping bag she nearly suffocated in the still canyon air. Over and over she wakened with a start, thinking it must be time to get up. No—not yet. Chuck had promised to shake her out of sleep the minute he was ready to start breakfast. Again she lapsed into an uneasy blur, half real, half dream.

Nice old Chuck. Glad it's Chuck and not Buzz I drew as a cooking partner. Good old voice behind me giving orders. "Back-paddle now. Easy does it. Fine—let 'er drift." Lately he had made Andy take the rear seat, getting her ready to ride the white water alone. Alone —lovely. Still—miss that voice.

The shuddery kiss from Buzz was not the only cause of Andrea's broken sleep. Tomorrow she would have to decide about Hell's Half Mile. She yearned to run it. But did it make sense? Yes—no—yes.

At campfire Ollie had taken *his* stand. "All two of my passengers are going to walk that piece of river," he said. "There's a genu-i-n-e drop off at the finish of Hell's Half. Remember it, Chuck?" Chuck nodded. "Well, it's no smaller this year. And right below is a gravel bar where like as not Buzz and me are going to get high-sanded." Some of you may catch it too. Better wear your second-best shoes tomorrow, Buzz," he added, his face still deadpan. "You might have to do a little walking on the river bottom."

Drowsily Andy wandered again through Chuck's speech, seeing the gnomelike figure distorted by grotesque shadows from the fire. "Hell's Half Mile is not exactly designed for foldboats," he was saying, "so get out and study the thing before you try it. There's a great big push of water going over great big rocks." Rocks—rocks everywhere. "A lot depends on how much flow there is. Three years ago when I was here, nobody even tried to go through. But it *has been run* in foldboats. One double and one single have made it. I know this particular rapid is something a lot of you hanker to try—certainly I do—but it's no disgrace to portage. We don't want any broken boats, or heads either." A broken boat —oh no—no. But *it has been run.*

When at last Chuck did come to shake her by the shoulder, Andy was groggy with sleep. She staggered up, dragged on her jeans, and tiptoed over the crackly leaves, trying not to disturb Martha and Finette. She was sure she had been awake all night. Yet the moon had vanished without her seeing it go. Now sunlight touched the tops of the cliffs, and before long it would be pouring heat into the whole canyon.

"Chuck, do you really think I ought to portage today?" Andy asked as she set out boxes of Shredded Wheat and Corn Flakes on a folding table.

Crouched at the edge of the fire, Chuck was turning bacon strips in an iron skillet. He looked up from his cooking, appraising his star pupil with gimlet eyes. "Pretty sure you should, Andy. You may have the know-how to handle your boat in that kind of water, but it also takes a lot of plain physical brawn to buck waves that size."

"Are you and Finette going to portage?" Andy asked. She poured water onto the powdered milk she had measured into a pitcher and turned to face him while she stirred the breakfast cream with unnecessary vim.

Again Chuck glanced up from the spitting bacon. "Finette's going to walk. No argument about that. I wouldn't dream of taking her." Then his microscope look changed to a twinkle. "Me—I'm just going to wait and see. Every year, and every month of the year, the water is different. According to Ollie, even the main channels change. Possibly Whit and I will join—— *Ouch!*" He dragged the pan away from the fire in a hurry. "That darned bacon fat spatters like a shotgun."

"I bet you don't portage," Andy said, a gleam in her own eyes.

"Don't be too sure. After all, I want to see that new car that's waiting for me in Detroit. You'll have to make your own decision, though, Andy. That's the price of being a solo foldboater. And you know enough to make the right one."

The discussion ended as hungry customers began to arrive, demanding oranges, or spooning applesauce into their cups from the big number-ten can on the table. Andy scurried about serving people and getting out more food. Chuck's confidence in her judgment was comforting. At the same time he had made it a responsibility—hers—not his.

When Connie appeared at breakfast he created a sensation. All over the top of his head great chunks of hair had been clipped right to the scalp. He looked as if a family of moths had been working on him all winter.

Mrs. Van Fleet screamed, "Connie! Darling!" and spilled her coffee.

"I don't know how it happened," Connie said in his

mild way. "I was asleep." Connie now not only looked
like a horse, but like a mangy horse.

"I'd certainly like to know who is responsible for
this outrage," his mother said grimly.

No one spoke up, but Andy had a fair idea who had
devised this senseless bit of humor.

All morning as she paddled down the river the question of portaging gnawed at the edges of Andrea's
mind. The proper way to approach such a decision, she
knew, was Chuck's way. Wait and see what the water
looks like. The trouble was she wanted so terribly to
run Hell's Half. For months the name had jumped out
at her from the map, a challenge as alluring as Circe
was to the companions of Ulysses. If she did portage
she certainly couldn't carry her boat alone. Whom
should she ask? Finette? A man would be a lot better.
Lance might offer to help, but she was not going to beg
for it. Not after last night.

The bald truth was Andrea Dawson didn't want to
portage. She wanted to run Hell's Half Mile. If she was
going to race from Salida to Cotopaxi someday she
ought to practice on every boiling stretch of water that
came her way.

And yet—and yet . . . The arguments spun in a circle. If she cracked up, if she wrecked her boat beyond
repair, then she would have to finish the trip riding the
raft with those deadly Van Fleets and, of all people,
Buzz. Buzz laughing at her, winking, cracking corny
jokes. Worse still, she would have to go home and face
her father. This boat was a gesture of trust from Dad,
a symbol that now she could take care of herself. If she
disappointed him—oh, he would still be kind—his
craggy face a mixture of kind and sorry which she
could not endure. Definitely nothing must happen to

the boat. The idea that she herself might be hurt played
no part in Andrea's thinking.

Today Ollie was leading the procession down the
river, and long before the familiar din of rough water
reached their ears he signaled his followers to pull off
onto a damp crescent of sand.

"Trail's on this side of the river," he told them, waving a chunky arm toward the mountain at their backs.
"Kind of up that hill and over some rocks and down
again. Matter of fact, she don't rightly look like a trail.
You'll just see tracks where folks have scrambled up and
down to get around the rapids, every fella for himself.
About the first place you can slide back to the river
again you'll get a good look at the big drop. Watch out
for cactus," he warned as Liz and Monk started off.
"You go lay your hand on a piece of that prickly pear,
crawling over rocks, and you ain't going to be very
happy holding a paddle for the next four-five days."

Suddenly it struck Andrea as she looked up the
trackless bank that for her there was more to this portage, or not to portage, business than the danger of the
river itself. If the trail was as steep and rough as it
sounded a girl with an unstable knee was going to have
a hard time scrambling over it. Let alone carrying one
end of a boat.

Full of misgivings, she started up through the brush
with the others. It was nervous going. Time after time
she stepped aside to let someone pass her on what Ollie
had accurately stated "don't rightly look like a trail."
It was slippery underfoot, steep, rocky, bristling with
cactus and fallen logs which had to be crawled over, or
detoured by climbing higher still on the side of the
mountain. To protect her knee from a sudden wrench
she moved slowly, clinging to branches of scrub
juniper, grasping at dead timber which often broke in
her hands.

The only person who did not pass Andrea was Mrs. Van Fleet. Propelled by her husband and dragged by her son, she was having a worse struggle with the trail than Andy. And all this time the river churned below, completely hidden by trees and brush.

If I injure this left knee getting down to the place where I can study the water, I really *will* be in a mess, Andy thought. A mess today—maybe for the rest of my life. That was the one stern warning all three doctors had given her. "Don't tear those ligaments loose a second time."

Abruptly Andrea made her decision. Right or wrong, she was going to run Hell's Half Mile. Chuck thought she ought to portage. That was clear from what he had said at breakfast, but something within kept telling her, "You can do it, Andy, you can do it." Either Chuck had forgotten, or never realized, how serious a bad twist could be. Not Chuck's fault, she told herself. For two years I've tried every minute of the time to hide the fact that there was anything wrong with my leg.

She sat down to rest until the Van Fleets moved out of sight. Then, working her way back down the difficult pitch even more cautiously than she had climbed up, Andy joined Ollie and Buzz at the boats.

One by one the walkers returned from scouting. "Well, Monk and I are certainly going to play it safe," Liz announced, sliding off the bank onto the sandspit.

Monk, close behind his long-legged wife, said, "We can't afford not to. For us it's plain dollars and cents. If we lose our boat this pretty little game will be over—for quite some time."

Even before she left camp that morning Martha had decided to portage. Tim was not a dependable paddler. No one said so, but by now everyone knew it. At times he did something almost brilliant. Then again, like yesterday, he lost his head completely.

"Give him five more years," Chuck had told her. "He's only a kid. Because his brain has grown up faster than his body, you forget how young he is."

Going to look at the rapids was a gesture—chiefly for Tim's morale. And having looked, it was easy to say, "This is not for us."

Lance, too, decided against the run, but for a reason quite different from Martha's. "I'd rather get a good movie of Johan swooping down Hell's Half than do it myself."

"You would?" Andy said wonderingly.

Lance looked at her down the length of his oversize nose. "Remember what you said once about the Dawson family?"

"That we're all nuts."

"That's right. Well, so am I."

"Suppose Johan decides he won't try it either?"

"In that case it's certainly not my meat. Anybody willing to give me a hand with my boat?"

"Glad to, Lance," Chuck said. "As soon as everybody gets organized. I'd like to study the layout once more before Whit and I take off."

"I knew it! I knew it!" Andy crowed. "Way back at breakfast I told you you'd never resist such a temptation."

"We came mighty close to resisting," Whit told her. "But for the two of us, I believe it's a sound gamble."

Johan was the next to get back. "She doesn't look impossible," he said crisply. "Anyhow, I try. You want I should go first, Chuck?"

Whit answered that one. "No argument, champ. It's all yours."

Taking a chocolate bar out of his pocket, Johan leaned against a rock, munching it as calmly as if he were about to ride the galloping horse on a merry-go-round.

Watching him, Andy thought, This is a different breed
from the rest of us—this Johan Speiser. He's not even
excited. I guess that's the way a champion has to be.

Last to reach the beach were Connie and his father.
"What's the news?" Chuck called out as Connie jumped
from the top of a ledge.

"I'm going to portage," Connie said quietly. "Mother
took one look at the rapids and burst into tears. Was
sure I'd be broken to bits if I tried it. So I've promised
to walk. Dad came back to help me carry, and I think
we'd better get started because Mother's terrified of
waiting alone in this 'utter wilderness,' as she calls it."

Slowly Connie moved toward his boat. His voice
was still patient, but he sounded tired. Mr. Van Fleet
picked up the other end of the boat and silence settled
over the River Runners as they watched the two men
start up the mountainside. No one spoke until they
were gone from sight.

"There's a really sweet guy," Martha said finally.

And Johan, quoting the old German proverb, crys-
tallized the thought in each person's heart. " 'Alles
verstehen ist alles vergeben,' we say in my country. 'To
understand all is to forgive all.' "

I'm not the only person in the world who has problems, Andy told herself. Perhaps, instead of worrying
about them, I should try to do something for Connie.

The oppressive stillness was broken and Chuck
moved swiftly back to business. "Well, we've heard
from everyone but you, Andy. Maybe Buzz will give
you a hand getting your boat over the hill.

"Me? Why, I'm going sailing," Andy announced jubilantly. She did not tell Chuck that she had never
reached the point where the trail came back to the
river so she could study the worst part of the rapids.
"And I'm going to travel right behind you and Whit—
I hope."

Chuck's jaw dropped in surprise, but he snapped it shut again without saying a word.

"Of course you're the leader, Chuck. You have a perfect right to insist that I portage."

The gimlet eyes had never looked at Andy more piercingly. "I told you to make your own decision. You have—so that's that."

Buzz stood up. "If Andy's going along with the crazy ones I might as well help you carry your boat Lance."

Looking at Timmie's slender shoulders, Lance said, "Better yet, Buzz, you take one end of Martha's boat and let Tim help me. Unless, of course, Chuck is absolutely bent on going downstream for another look at the water."

Chuck shook his head. "Negative. To be truthful, one trip up and down that billy-goat slide, carrying Whit's boat, is all I want in a day. We won't put into the water till you get back, Buzz, so the raft can be close behind us. That'll give us a chance, also, to hash over the details, rock by rock before we start."

Andy understood what Chuck meant. She was going to get the briefing of her life on how to run Hell's Half.

Surprisingly, Andy found she was not nervous. Her muscles did not pull tight or her stomach twist into a knot. She was exhilarated, and within her was the conviction that whatever she needed to do she would be able to do.

As she moved down the river her senses seemed to grow more alert, her body actually stronger. "Just old nature pouring a little adrenalin into your blood," Chuck would have said. "That stuff she holds back for emergencies." Whether it was adrenalin or the sheer joy of "water-flying" Andy didn't know. She knew it was wonderful.

Sitting low in the water, feeling its every throb and

quiver, being hurled along by the river while all the
time you were making your boat go where your ears
and eyes told you it ought to go—this was ecstasy—or
madness—or both.

Water dashed against boulders with a cannonade
that echoed from one wall of the canyon to the other.
Andy's glance flicked birdlike from side to side, reading the crests of foam as her tiny shell was whirled
along. She leaned a little left, a little right. The boat
responded like a live thing. For Andy, at that instant,
it *was* a live thing with a mind and soul of its own.

Then she no longer had time to watch anything except the exact spot where she was paddling, the span
of water just ahead. The waves were growing bigger,
the rocks harder to dodge. Johan was some distance
ahead, but she could still see his back, upright in the
center of the narrow slalom boat. She dared not lift her
eyes to look at him for more than a fraction of a second,
for every paddle stroke was becoming an emergency,
something to be battled through and conquered. And
she was conquering. Today she was unbeatable.

The noise of the water grew deafening. The final
drop must be coming quickly now. She strained to see
whether Chuck and Whit were choosing the right or
left of an enormous boulder. It was a point they had not
been able to decide positively in advance. She caught
one clear view of their boat veering left. Then they dis-
appeared over the edge and spray blotted out every
trace of them. Andy followed, for in this avalanche
there was no turning back. Her boat catapulted into
a dive. "Water pony buck heap much," the Indians had
said. Heap much is right, Andy thought as, blind with
water, she held her breath until she felt the bow begin
to rise. Surely, steadily, it came up out of the hole. She
had it made. *Made!*

A grinding jolt raked the bottom of the boat, slewed

her sharply out of line. For one long horrible instant
Andrea felt the roots of her hair prickle as she fought
to drag herself out of the rocking trough. If the boat
turned broadside in this Niagara, it would swamp immediately. I must have hit a rock, she thought numbly.
I wonder if Chuck hit it too. Well, it can't have made
much of a hole, or I'd be under the water by now.

Gradually the pace of the river slackened. Ahead she
saw the gravel bar Ollie had mentioned, and there on a
stony flat were people—marvelous people—and foldboats—and Lance, with his movie camera, grinding
away.

Johan, as well as Chuck and Whit, was sweeping on
downstream, but Andrea felt tired. She pulled in to the
bank both to rest and to inspect for damage. Tim and
Finette came running to help her ashore.

"Oh, Andy," Finette cried, folding her in a bear hug,
"now I *know* you're crazy."

Tim said, "Gosh! What a trip!"

"Here comes the raft," Lance yelled, and they
watched enthralled as it came humping over the drop
like a great black caterpillar.

As soon as the photographic excitement ended Lance
joined them. "What a recovery!" he exulted. "I thought
it was all over. And then by some miracle you straight-
ened out again."

"I think I hit a rock," Andy said. "It felt as if something came up out of the river and smacked me. And
it wasn't any fish, either."

Lance helped her turn the boat upside down on the
smooth water-worn stones. There was a gash on the bottom all right, but not a large one. Even more fortunately, it had not cut all the way through the hull.

The big moment was over. Hell's Half was behind
them and the little crowd began putting boats into the

water. Finette was taking Whit's boat the rest of the way alone.

"Good luck," Andy called as she picked up the paddle."

"I'm glad it isn't far," Finette called back.

A loud bellow from the middle of the river made both Lance and Andrea look up. The raft had grounded on the gravel bar. Buzz went over the side and stood knee-deep in the current, pushing with all his bull strength against the stern. The raft did not budge.

"I bet Buzz hates that job," Lance said, wiping a hot hand over his own forehead.

"I don't understand Buzz," Andy said suddenly. She didn't quite know why she was saying this to Lance. The words just came out. Perhaps she was excited because she had run Hell's Half and made it right side up. It was as if somewhere back there in the rapids she had left behind that tightly curled up ball of shyness which had lodged inside her for so many years whenever she tried to talk to a boy.

"Some of the things Buzz wants are exactly the things I want most. Only for him it's football and for me it's foldboating. To be good at them, I mean. And yet——" She hesitated, groping for the words to express her feeling. "Buzz doesn't add up right."

"Does anybody understand anybody?" Lance asked seriously.

"Perhaps not."

They waved at Buzz as he struggled to dislodge the black monster, but it was Ollie who waved back. "Maybe I should wade out and give him a hand," Lance said. "Everyone else has left." But before he made up his mind to do it, Buzz drove one shoulder against the mass of neoprene as if he had been tackling a tiger, and the raft floated away.

Andy turned back to examine the tear in her boat. "I suppose I better get out my patching kit," she sighed.

"Let's use mine. It's easier than turning your boat
right side up again. A temporary job ought to last out
today. We haven't far to go." Lance went to his own
boat and came back with a repair box.

Andrea had not noticed before the lithe way in which
Lance walked. He was not a muscular person, but he
moved without effort, as if there might be a coiled
steel spring inside of him. His fingers, too, were quick
and deft. Even in such a simple operation as cutting
off pieces of yellow adhesive tape and plastering it on
the bottom of the boat, there was no waste motion.

"There," he said, smoothing the surface of the hull.
"After we make camp I'll do a permanent one for you."

"You're awfully kind, Lance," Andy said, meaning
it. "We River Runners work on the theory of every fellow for himself. Unless somebody's in real trouble, of
course. I'm not used to all this service."

"That's why it's fun to do things for you," Lance
told her. "You don't take them for granted."

Still they sat there on the stones, waiting for something, although there was nothing to wait for. Lance
pulled the dregs of a package of Crystomints out of
his pocket and offered her one.

"Mm! A party," Andy said, accepting it gratefully.

She thought she had never been so happy. She had
run the most difficult water they would meet on the
trip. Not perfectly, but without serious damage. Lance
said she had made a wonderful recovery after hitting
the rock. She knew she had. It was a close thing, touch
and go for a couple of seconds. She realized now what
Chuck had meant about needing brawn as well as
know-how.

And now Lance was sitting here beside her because
he wanted to. He didn't have to stay. Yesterday's ugly
moment with Buzz faded out of mind as she basked in
the warm approval of this friendly long-legged boy.

CHAPTER NINE

Early in the afternoon the River Runners made their camp at Rippling Brook, which at this season of the year was no brook at all but a dry wash slicing sharply between red sandstone cliffs. At the foot of the bluff a narrow flat spattered with cottonwood trees gave ample space for fifteen people to spread their beds in comfort and privacy. Behind this belt of green the bold vermilion wall climbed skyward in massive ledges.

"Look, Timmie!" Martha cried as she stepped out of their boat. "A staircase for giants." Still holding the paddle in her hand, she stood motionless, her defiant little chin uptilted in wonder. Patches of juniper had rooted somehow on the lower benches. Higher up, with nature's miraculous instinct for each different life zone, the juniper vanished and Douglas fir appeared.

"Why, it's a hanging garden," Martha exulted. "Do you suppose the hanging gardens of Babylon were as stunning as this? 'By the rivers of Babylon there we sat down,' " she chanted. "But this gang isn't going to do any weeping like the poor Israelites." Martha laid one arm fondly across Tim's shoulders. "Like it?" Tim nodded and smiled into his mother's eyes even as he jerked away.

Lance, too, stood on the pebbly beach letting his photographer's eye sweep the brilliant backdrop. "It would take a wide-angle lens to catch the feeling of this," he said wistfully. "I'd better stick with my fauna."

"You'll just have to remember it," Andy told him.

"Don't think I won't. As a matter of fact, I carry around a whole suitcase of landscape paintings—in my head. This will be one of them, I think. Anytime I feel a touch low all I have to do is take out my paintings, one at a time, and look at them. No charge for excess baggage."

"May I see your etchings someday?" Andy flashed, startled at her own daring.

Lance grinned. "Might take quite a while to look at all of them."

The big raft nosed ashore just then and Lance went to give Buzz a hand with unloading. Then, pulling his own bag from the stack of canvas sausages on the beach, he plunged an arm into the middle of it, came up with his binoculars. Long legs dangling, he perched on the rim of the raft to study the cliffs through power eyes.

"Seen your golden eagle yet?" Andy asked as she struggled her own bag out of the pile.

Without moving his eyes from the binoculars, Lance shook his head. "Not even a feather. Not even an old nest. Nothing but hawks. There's a doe up there on the mountain, staring at us. Probably wondering what business we have on her property. There she goes— white flag flying! Must be fun to leap through the trees that way."

One by one the boats were lifted ashore and a feeling of jubilee filled the air. The big bad bogey was behind them now, and they needed a celebration.

"Look," Liz cried, pointing down the beach. "There's our mascot." All eyes followed her finger to the bleached skeleton of a female mountain sheep. "Come on, Monk. Let's turn the old girl right side up and dress her for a gala."

"Used to be big bands of wild sheep running on these cliffs," Ollie told them. "I shot one not far from here 'long about—umm——" He squinted his eyes up in the effort of recollection. "About twenty-five years ago. Too bad they didn't turn this country into a National Monument before all the sheep were cleaned out."

They christened the mascot with warm brown river water, named her Cleopatra, queen of the Nile. Liz filched Chuck's straw hat for her head, decorated it with a garland of cottonwood leaves, and draped the gaunt white ribs in a plaid shirt and bandannas. During the whole lazy afternoon Cleopatra was a gathering place for tea drinking and snack nibbling. She lent an air of festival to the entire camp.

Back from the river, in shallow caves cut by flood water at the base of the soft sandstone mountain, they found other skeletons. Ribs and leg bones were scattered about, relics of deer perhaps, which had found refuge during a storm or been dragged there to make a leisurely meal for one of the big mountain cats.

Andy began tossing out some old white bones to spread her sleeping bag in one of these rock shelters. But Finette's discovery of a large working anthill in the middle of what was about to be her bed made her change her mind in a hurry. They chose instead a little circle of ground covered with dry grass and screened by cottonwoods.

"No caves for me," Martha said. "I like to sleep straight under the stars." She gave another blow at the valve of her air mattress, paused for breath. "This is a perfect camp, isn't it? Cliffs behind us to break the wind and the river so close we can almost reach out in the night to dip up a drink of water." With a comfortable sigh she stretched herself on the mattress to test the amount of air in it. "Perfect," she announced. "I think I'll stay right here until tomorrow morning."

"Tired, Martha?" Finette asked. "Want me to make you a cup of tea?"

"Maybe I am tired," Martha said thoughtfully. "That portage was a toughie." Andy bobbed her head in agreement. "But I think I'm just let down." Martha lifted both arms into the air and let them fall again, limp as string. "I can't help wondering whether I was wrong to bring Tim on this trip. Kids do have to follow their own stars. Perhaps I'm trying to push Tim into my orbit. Tell me honestly, you two. Am I being a Mrs. Van Fleet?"

"You!" Finette and Andy chorused the word.

"I'm sort of glad Mrs. V. came along," Finette said. "It will make me, at least, more patient with Connie and his prissy ways."

"You know," Andy said meditatively, "until this trip I never thought much about my parents. Never thought about them *as* parents, I mean. Whether they were good ones or bad ones."

"Possibly because you've never been so far away from them before," Martha told her.

Finette said gently, "I know they're good ones."

"Good! They're divine! I ought to begin every day saying, 'Thank you, God, for giving me a mother and father who take care of me when I need it and shove me out to flap my own wings when I need that.' Oh, they're special!"

Still mulling over Connie's problems, Finette said, "I've read about these fragile, fainting moms who keep their children on a leash forever, but I never ran into one before."

Martha sat up so quickly she lost her balance and rolled off the mattress onto the grass. "Well, nobody

ever called me fragile," she said, laughing. "And I've
never fainted in my life. Also, there's no use stewing
about whether Tim should or should not have come.
He's here. One does the best one knows at the time—
and who can do more?" Briskly she stood up. "One
thing I do know. Having Lance with us has been wonderful. Lance is everything Timmie would like to be,
and camping right beside him is the thrill of his life."

"Lance is nice," Andy said. "He's going to help me
vulcanize my boat this afternoon."

Martha chuckled to herself. "Until this summer I
hadn't seen Lance since he graduated from high school.
He's really been glued together since then."

"Glued together?" Andrea's wide-set eyes grew puzzled. "I don't get it."

"No-o. I don't suppose you do, Andy. What I mean
is, two years ago he still had that colt look—all legs
and a face which hadn't quite grown up to his nose.
That doesn't really explain the change either. He's
jelled, that's all. His mind and his body and his manners have all reached the same stage of grown-upness."

"My father is always raving about people with 'the
nose of energy,'" Andy said. "We tease him about it at
home. Tell him he's throwing out a big smoke screen to
cover up for his own oversize nose."

"Lance doesn't look a bit out of proportion now,"
Finette said.

"No, he really doesn't." Martha cocked her head to
one side, as if she could consider her nephew more
objectively in that position. "Though he still reminds
me of a heron occasionally. All legs and beak. Especially when he's stalking something with that camera
of his."

"You're mean to your nephew," Andy wailed. "I
think he's beautiful. I shall blackmail you by threaten-
ing to tell Lance what Aunt Martha said about him."

"Lance is so busy doing the things he's doing I don't believe he'd give a whoop and a holler what Aunt Martha called him."

While they talked Andy had been rummaging in her duffel bag, stirring the contents like a pudding. She came up now with a faded, rumpled, and none too clean cotton shirt. "Look at this thing," she moaned. "Why didn't I have sense enough to buy some fresh shirts for this expedition? Mother begged me to, but I told her there were no holes in the old ones so why worry. Do you suppose this would dry before dinner if I washed it now?"

Finette flicked back a cuff to look at her waterproof watch. "I don't suppose any such thing. Want to wear one of mine tonight?"

"Are you serious?" Andy's jaw dropped. "Would it fit me?"

"Of course I'm serious. And seriously, your clothes are a disgrace, Andy. My selling eye tells me my shirt will fit you because what I take up in front you'll take up in the shoulders." Finette slid back the long side zipper on her bag, lifted out a carefully folded green and white checked shirt. It was ironed and spotless.

"But can you spare it?" Andy gasped, overcome at such generosity. "How many shirts did you bring?"

"Seven. Just one a day."

Andy buried her face in her hands. "You make me blush. I brought two. One to get wet and one to wear while the other was drying."

Martha giggled. "You're as bad as Tim, Andy."

"Well, clothes are a chore. Only sometimes . . ." The sentence hung unfinished as almost reverently Andy laid Finette's shirt on top of the muddle in her dunnage. "I shan't put it on until I've finished working on the boat. I ought to clean out the inside too, and when I finish with that I'll look like a chimney sweep."

"You'll never look like a chimney sweep," Martha told her. "But you *could* use a hairbrush. Even before you go down to work on your boat. If I had golden-corn hair like yours I'd brush it until people could use it for a mirror."

Andy compromised by dipping a pocket comb into the river and whisking it over her head. "Got to skoot now. Lance is meeting me on the beach at four."

Lance was waiting for her, chinning with Ollie meanwhile as the boatman painted some tarry substance over the new gravel scuffs on the bottom of the raft.

"Makes me feel better about running onto a rock to see you in the repair shop too, Ollie," Andy called out.

Carefully Ollie daubed another layer over the deepest gash. "That's the old Green for you," he said philosophically. "Different every week of every year. But there wouldn't be any kick in it if we just sailed over smooth water. Might as well truck freight up and down the Mississippi."

With Lance's help, patching the foldboat was easy. A new keel strip was not necessary, and Lance applied the self-vulcanizing cement with swift fingers.

Before he finished, Buzz came down to the river in swimming trunks, stood watching with a rather pleased expression on his face.

"You really caught one, didn't you, Miss Spitfire?" Buzz said.

"Not bad," Lance said without looking up.

"Must say you had your nerve with you shooting that place." Buzz tossed a piece of chewed-out gum into the bushes and waded into the stream. Waist-deep, he threw himself against the current, his great arms flailing like steel pistons.

"When the cement is dry I'd better do a little house-keeping," Andy said. "I haven't mopped out the sand and stuff on the bottom since we left Brown's Park."

"Seems like a long time ago—Brown's Park. Doesn't it?" Lance stared at her speculatively, and Andy realized what Martha meant by his heron look. "I remember watching your face that day as you put your boat together. I thought I'd never seen a girl so intent on anything. Right away I liked you because you were more interested in what you were doing than in how you looked or who was looking at you."

"It certainly seems as if I'd known you more than a few days."

"That's wilderness for you, Andy. One reason for going into it. Gives you the illusion of living through more time."

"You want more time?" The dead weight of hours which had hung over her between Black Saturday and the day she started foldboating swept Andy's mind.

"But of course. Doesn't everybody? There's so much to do. I'll never see all the rivers or take all the pictures or know all the people I'd like to know."

Lance tossed philosophy into the air as abruptly as he had plunged into it. He grabbed Andy's hand as she was about to turn the boat right side up again. "Don't waste this lovely afternoon housekeeping, Andy. Let's go swimming."

Andy couldn't resist the invitation. He really wants to go swimming with *me*, she thought. Not just go swimming. To mop the bottom of the boat was not really essential. It was merely that Andrea was as careful about the appearance of her boat as she was casual about her own. Anyhow, she decided, If I get up early tomorrow morning I can do it before we start.

"Here are my good resolutions," she said, holding out upturned palms toward Lance. "Take them away and bury them while I get into my suit."

Andrea went to sleep that night drenched in happi-

ness. It was not happiness about any particular thing.
Lance had not said anything or done anything to cause
such an upsurge. He had merely given her his friendship—a comfortable gift—and in accepting it she felt
comfortable. For the first time since the days of skiing
with Don she sat relaxed, talking with a boy. With
Lance there was no struggle to dream up a subject for
conversation. Even silence lay easily between them.
She wished the river trip were going to be longer. She
wished Lance lived in San Francisco. Oh, if wishes were
horses Andrea Dawson would have quite a ride.

Still, there would be those wonderful days of driving
from Utah to California in Martha's car. She and Lance
would eat breakfast together, watch the desert colors
together, the cloud shapes, sunsets, moonrise—she drifted
off into delicious sleep.

A sharp rattling noise brought her stark awake. Startled, she sat bolt upright in her sleeping bag. What time
was it? Midnight or 4 A.M.? There! It came again. The
racket was on the cliff above her head. Some animal
scrambling around up there must have kicked some
pebbles loose. Andy listened intently. No sound now
except her own heartthrob, Finette's soft breathing.
Then a rock came rattling down. She reached into one
of the shoes parked beside her bed to get a flashlight,
turned the beam up the cliff to scare away whatever
was knocking down loose debris.

At the same instant Finette sat up too. "What is it,
Andy? Can you see anything?"

"Not a thing. I think a rock came rolling down the
cliff, but I only heard it. Didn't actually see it land."

The next crash brought all three of them to their feet.
Three beams of light patterned the ledges above their
heads.

"What on earth?" Martha muttered as she turned her

flash on the ground around their beds. "Could a deer
be raising all that rumpus?"

"Sounds more like a buffalo," Finette whispered.

The glare of Martha's light came to rest on a rock as
big as a grapefruit lying between Finette's bed and her
own. "I know that wasn't there when we made our beds
this afternoon. There was nothing here but grass."

"It certainly wasn't." Finette almost hissed the words.

Another rock came bounding down the bluff, hitting
from ledge to ledge, rolling with such force that it went
all the way to the edge of the river.

"Quick," Martha said. "Grab a sweater or something
and let's get back into the trees till the avalanche
stops."

Then they heard a laugh, a smothered undercover
laugh, but still the unmistakable haw-haw-haw which
could come from only one person.

"Why, that's Buzz up there," Andy gasped. "He's
rolling rocks down onto us."

"Oh, Andy, no! He couldn't be. Not purposely."
Martha sounded shocked.

"Oh, couldn't he though!" Andy shot back. "That
Buzz has a weird sense of humor."

Martha called out as loudly as she dared. After all,
she did not wish to waken the entire camp. "Buzz! Buzz!
Is that you up there?"

There was no reply except another muted haw-haw
and a bigger chunk of sandstone rocketing toward them.

"It *is* Buzz." Martha was outraged. "Buzz, you come
down off those ledges this minute before you kill somebody. Do you hear me?"

Andy edged close against Finette as they retreated
into the trees. Martha still stood at the foot of the cliff.

"Why is he doing this, Finette?" Andy begged. "I
don't understand. Does he really think it's funny? Or
is he trying to get even with me because I wouldn't

stand for his pawing the other night?" Andy shivered. "I'd as soon be embraced by a gorilla."

Martha ran back to the trees where the two girls were huddled. "Do either of you know where Chuck's bed is? I'm going to waken him."

"I haven't the vaguest notion," Finette said.

"Nor I."

"Well, where does Ollie sleep? It can't be far unless he sleeps in the river."

"I saw Ollie carrying his stuff down to the far sand-spit. Way beyond where Cleo is."

"Well, it's Chuck I want anyhow. I'll just have to prowl around until I find him. Ollie's too good-natured. It's time somebody taught that oaf up there the rudiments of manners." She bent to tie her Keds. "This is the most outrageous piece of horseplay—if it is horse-play—I ever heard of in my life."

Martha vanished into the blackness. The other two stood waiting, watching the flicker of Martha's flash come and go between the trees. A branch cracked loudly. Out on the river a bird called through the dark. They extinguished their lights and stood locked together, waiting through eternity until the tiny beam of Martha's flash began coming toward them again.

She clicked it off as she reached them. "I couldn't find Chuck anywhere. All sleeping bags look alike in the dark and men apparently sleep with their heads buried under the covers."

Finette giggled. "Connie doesn't." But Martha was not in a mood to joke.

Andy asked, "What time is it? How long till daylight?"

"Not long. Half an hour at most," Martha told her.

"Oh, Martha, what do you think we ought to do?"

"I knew where Tim was sleeping, so I wakened Lance. I thought surely he would know which tree

Chuck had picked. But he didn't. Instead Lance insisted on going after Buzz himself. Said he could deal with him better than Chuck could."

Andy felt a surge of horror. She had herself been in the grip of those arms. The memory clung.

"I certainly take a dim view of that," Martha sputtered, "but I couldn't talk him out of it."

"Let's hope Lance doesn't follow the rocks," Finette said between her teeth.

"I imagine my nephew can look after himself, but I'm not mad for the idea of his wrestling with Buzz up there in the juniper. And if Buzz doesn't choose to come down, Lance certainly can't make him. Oh, I wish I could have found Chuck. He's the leader of this outfit."

" 'In all that the Law leaveth open, the word of the Head Wolf is Law,' " Finette quoted under her breath.

"Too close to the jungle for me," Martha retorted, still angry at such senseless behavior.

In her thin pajamas Andy shivered. The shivering came from within, like a premonition of disaster.

"Think we should get back into bed?" Finette asked. "Andy's quaking like an aspen."

"Well, I'm certainly not going to sleep out there in the target area until I know our assistant boatman has come down to my level." Martha's words came in jerks, still hot with indignation. "That idiot. He might have killed one of us. If he kicked those rocks loose accidentally it was unpardonably careless. If this is one of Buzz's jests . . ." She left her idea of suitable punishment unuttered as they swooped up their sleeping bags and retreated again to the shelter of the trees.

They piled the three bags on top of each other and sat on them, close together, waiting, listening, jumping at every cricket chirp or small crackle out of the night.

"Daylight's coming," Finette said after a particularly long silence.

Martha said, "So is Christmas."

"No, I mean it. The sky is only pewter color now instead of black."

Andy was unable to speak at all. Over and over she kept wondering, Is this something that I have done? Is Buzz trying to get back at me? Or is he up there chasing gophers or whatever people like Buzz chase? Suppose Lance gets hurt. Oh, don't let him get hurt!

"Look! There's a light up on the cliff." Martha pointed excitedly. All three strained to follow the pinpoint as it came and went in the blackness, then vanished completely. "Lance must be climbing up."

Again they waited. The change in the color of the sky grew plain to all of them. "My stars are going to bed," Martha said. "They don't like these goings on." A hail of loose rock stopped her short. They could hear voices now—two voices—but the words were indistinguishable. Two beams of light appeared, moved, were lost again in the brush.

"How long has it been since Lance started?" Andy whispered, the sound wrung from her throat.

"Too long," Martha said, tightening her arm around Andy's shoulder. "But I think they must be coming down. I saw a light quite close above us."

Suddenly there was a thud on the ground and through the slowly increasing light Andy saw Lance standing where her bed had been. He must have jumped the last few feet. His back was toward her, as he intently watched the cliff above him.

"Come on down, Buzz. This is where the girls' camp is." Lance's voice was not loud, but it carried authority. "We made an agreement and if you know what's good for you, you'll stick to it." This was a new Lance. Stern, almost hard. A different person from the boy who spent an hour watching a sandpiper limp up and down the beach to disguise her nesting place. Another thud and Buzz landed beside Lance.

Martha walked quickly toward them. "What in the name of common sense were you trying to do, Buzz? Kill somebody?" She pointed a scornful finger at the biggest piece of stone, visibly red now in the growing dawn.

"I didn't mean to hurt anybody," Buzz growled. "That Andy's so high-hat I wanted to give her a good scare, that's all."

Lance said, "Come on, Buzz. Get going."

Buzz glared at Lance. "Okay then. I'm sorry."

"That's no apology. You make it to all three of them and make it right." Lance moved a step closer to Buzz.

"You didn't say how *many* people I had to apologize to."

"Maybe I didn't specify, but you know darn well what I meant. Either I go straight to Chuck now with the whole story or . . ."

Buzz put his hands on his hips in a mock ladylike gesture. "Bring on your women. Maybe you'd like me to go down on my knees."

Martha walked back into the trees, returned with Andy and Finette. "Buzz wants to apologize to us," she said as the three stood arm in arm before him.

The surly look on Buzz's face was anything but penitent. "I'm sorry if I scared you so bad," he mumbled. "Thought it would be a good joke on Andy. Hope you'll excuse it." Buzz turned back to face Lance. "Satisfied?"

"I suppose so," Lance said in a low voice. "Perhaps that's the best apology you know how to make."

"You're satisfied then that I've done what I said I'd do? And you aren't going to blab a big bunch of hogwash to Chuck?"

"Not if you stick to your rowing from here in. No

more haircutting or rock rolling or any other capers you
might dream up."

"Okay then." Buzz moved in close to Lance. "I've
done what I said I'd do. Now I'll settle with you—you
bird-chasing twerp!" He made a lunge toward Lance
as if to tear him apart. But Lance was not there. He
stepped aside so swiftly that Buzz went lunging past
him at thin air.

"Oh no! Not this too." Andy stood biting her fingers
to keep her teeth from chattering.

"If you want to pick a fight with me why don't you
come out and say so?" Lance said evenly. He spread
his feet slightly apart as if to grip the ground more
solidly, watched every movement of the burly body
confronting him.

"Brother, you're going to wish you'd never left
Oregon before I get through with you," Buzz rumbled,
gathering himself for another spring.

"Wouldn't you rather fight over on the grass?" Lance
said. "It'll be softer for you when you fall." Swiftly he
moved to the trampled space where the three sleeping
bags had been spread at the very edge of the water.

Purpling at the insult, Buzz came after him. Andy
felt Martha's body go rigid. Buzz reached for Lance,
and Andy expected to see him pounded to mincemeat
by those big fists. But it didn't happen. It was hard to
see what did happen, because it was all over so fast.
Buzz's enormous body went hurtling over Lance's
shoulder and landed in the river with a high splash.

The horrible tension that had gripped the girls when
the fight began shattered as Buzz hit the water. It was
like the comedian throwing custard pie in the villain's
face. It was the funniest thing that had ever happened
in the world. Buzz floundered in the water, struggled
to his feet, stumbled on the slippery bottom, and sat
down again. They rocked with laughter. They forgot

about wakening other people. They stood on the edge
of the river shrieking with mirth until tears ran down
their faces. They doubled up with laughter, and Buzz,
finding his feet at last, stood in the river, water stream-
ing from his hair and clothes. In him was no mirth at
all. To be laughed at was worse than being beaten at
his own game. With a final scowl at his convulsed audience, Buzz threw himself back into the water and swam
out of sight around the corner of the beach.

Martha was first to find her voice. "I don't understand. How did you do it? That hulk. You sent him
spinning like a pebble."

Lance grinned, his deadly grimness gone. "He wasn't
expecting it, that's all."

"Come on, that's not all."

"Well, it's too early in the morning for a lecture on
judo, Aunt Martha."

"Judo! Where on earth did you pick that up?"

"At home. We've had a Japanese university student
as houseboy the last couple of years. He wears the judo
brown belt, which means he's quite good, and he's
taught me a fair amount about it too. It's terrific exer-
cise and apparently can be handy too."

"But Buzz is so much bigger than you are." Martha
refused to let the subject drop.

"Size has nothing to do with it. Balance and technique are what count. Roughly the idea is to give way
to force at first until you sense your opponent's weakness. Then . . ." Lance lifted one shoulder to show
what should happen to an opponent's weakness. "What
I did to Buzz is called the shoulder wheel. Just one of
dozens of ways judo has for dealing with a bigger person. You should see Totso toss me through the air. And
he's a little bit of a guy. Well—I'd better be running
along. Everybody in camp must be awake after all this
foofooraw."

Lance strode off through the trees and Andy watched, seeing him in a whole new dimension.

The sun was not yet high enough to reach its warm fingers into the canyon, but daylight had definitely come. And in Andy's heart, as she sat cross-legged on her sleeping bag, brushing her hair to make it shine—like a mirror this time—there was also a new glow.

CHAPTER TEN

That morning Andy floated down to the beach on invisible wings. She had planned to get up early to clean out the inside of her boat, though not as early as daybreak. Still, the extra time would let her do a thorough job. She dragged out everything under the deck—paddles, spray cover, Mae West, the repair kit, seat cushion, rubber sponge, an extra hat, old rags, a waterproof bag of cheese and Triscuit—and finally the two inflated rubber tires stuffed into the boat fore and aft.

This cleanup is definitely overdue, she thought as she sponged mud off the spray cover and hung it on a bush to dry. Why did I put it off so long? But this morning she didn't mind house cleaning. She could have swept a cobbled street and liked it. While she worked she hummed one of those tuneless ditties which gave her so much satisfaction and Marianne so much pain.

After all removable objects had been wiped she crawled under the deck on her stomach to mop the bottom. Abruptly the song stopped and a wail came from within.

Andy ran her finger along the central longeron, hoping that what she saw was a shadow, a bad dream which would go away when she touched it. But her fingernail gave the lie to that. This was no dream. She was looking at a crack in the main longitudinal brace of her boat. Not a wide crack, but at least six inches long. How deeply it had bitten into the wood was anybody's guess. No need to ask how it happened. The break was directly over the spot which Lance had vulcanized. The longeron had split when she hit the rock in Hell's Half.

Waves of confusion and worry raced each other through Andrea's brain. She ought to tell Chuck about this. And what would he say? He might say, "Pack up your boat and finish the trip on the raft. Why take a chance with only two more days to go?" Andy shuddered. Finish the trip on that scow? Ride with Buzz for two days? No and *no*. That she could never bring herself to do. Even before today it would have been sad to sit with Buzz and the Van Fleets, but after the ducking Lance had given him this morning, Buzz would be intolerable. He'd find some horrible way to get back at her.

She debated asking Lance if he knew of a way to repair the crack. She did not doubt that Lance would do it for her if means could be found, but he might discuss it with Chuck. And old safety-first Chuck, with his enormous sense of responsibility for others, would not approve of any mended longeron. She peered at it again. It wasn't much of a crack, really. Just a tiny break, scarcely wide enough to get a fingernail into. This morning—this sunny, singing morning—nothing could be very wrong.

"I do it mine ownself," Andrea muttered, backing out to get a roll of mending tape from the beach. She wound carefully, round and round, pulling the adhesive tight and straight. She laid extra pieces longitudinally to reinforce the first wrapping. "After all, doctors sometimes set bones in adhesive, so why should-

n't my boat have a cast of tape?" she demanded of the
morning air. The air made no answer.

Once more song began to bubble from her lips.

"And dashing and flashing and splashing and clashing;
And so never ending, but always descending,
All at once and all o'er, with a mighty uproar,
And this way the water comes down at Lodore."

She crammed the tires into place, packed away the
other articles, and, happy as any housewife with spring
cleaning behind her, hurried off toward the place
under the cottonwoods where a lovely smell of wood
smoke mingled with the even lovelier smell of fried ham.

Andrea had been awake nearly four hours. She had
lived through falling rocks, the suspense of wondering
if Lance also would roll down the cliff, and finally a
judo contest. She was really ready for breakfast.

Cruising down the river was never more blissful than
on this morning which had started so strangely. The
little blue foldboat had come to be almost a second skin
to Andrea. The paddle, which once seemed a clumsy
piece of wood to be manipulated with concentrated
thought, moved now as if it were part of her arms.

Lance kept his boat near hers most of the time.
Where the river ran lazily they paddled side by side.
When the drumming of white water sounded in their
ears they took turns leading the way through tumbling
riffles and whirlpools laced with foam.

Andy knew she was paddling better than she had
ever paddled in her life. Today everything seemed to
click. Perhaps it was the steady practice of the past
week which had upped her skill into a new bracket, or
perhaps it was because she knew Lance was watching
with approving eyes. Whatever the reason, her judgment seemed swift and sure, her balance smooth as a
circus rider's.

When Steamboat Rock loomed up ahead she could scarcely believe they had come so far. Seen first from the side, this mighty headland did indeed look like a great buff-colored battleship. From the front it reminded her vaguely of El Capitan in Yosemite Valley. Though Andy was not one to remember mathematical dimensions, it seemed far bigger than El Capitan. Possibly it was this morning's mood of intensification, etching every leaf and bubble more sharply on her consciousness, that made this massive cliff so overpowering. Perhaps it was because she came so close to the base of the rock, measuring it against her tiny self. El Capitan she had seen only from an automobile, whisking past on a paved road. But today she was part of the river swirling past the vast headland.

Here at Steamboat Rock they met the Yampa, which they had crossed long ago on the day they rode from Vernal to Brown's Park. The Yampa looked far greener than the Green. "Geography in books doesn't make sense," Andy murmured. "You have to see it, be in the middle of it." Even after the Yampa joined the Green it kept to itself for a time, running along the south bank in a separate ribbon, untouched by the murky water coming down from Lodore.

Lodore is my canyon, Andy thought. Our canyon. Lance's and mine, because he feels the magic of it too, the way the Indians felt magic there. Only they thought it was wicked magic, and we know it's wonderful. If you love a piece of wilderness enough it actually gets to be yours. And Lodore is safe now. Nobody can dam it up or take it away from the people to whom it really belongs.

Steamboat Rock had already been photographed from every possible angle, but Lance had to make his own try. After lunch in Echo Park, directly across the river, he and Andy wandered up an old dirt road to a point where he thought he could catch the whole promontory in his lens.

Looking down on Echo Park from above, Lance said, "I'd like to come back here in October when the trees are yellow. What a picture that would make."

"I think it's perfect now," Andy told him.

Jones Hole tonight would be their last river home. It was bittersweet for Andy to think that the trip she had looked forward to so long was about to end. Sweet to think of a hot bath and a bed with freshly ironed sheets and a tall glass of milk. Bitter to realize that next week Lance would be gone from her life. It was sweet to know that they were planning to spend an extra day at Jones Hole, resting and exploring the canyon where ancient Indian people had left pictographs painted on the rock.

Also at Jones Hole, Ollie had promised them two things. A stream of clear, ice-cold water to drink from and, on the last evening, a barbecue. Via the road into Echo Park, Ollie had arranged to have a whole fresh lamb brought in. He himself would cook it, and Chuck talked about the way Ollie barbecued a roast until he had them all drooling. The whole last day danced ahead of Andy like a fried-chicken picnic out of her childhood.

The trail which led to the pictographs ran back from the river and along the edge of Jones Creek. This was no rock climb, so Andy was able to take it without worrying about her knee. For her, the walk was made even pleasanter by the fact that Buzz decided to go fishing. Earlier in the season he had gone to see what he described as "a few kid scrawls," and nothing, he maintained, "But nothing, would get me to hike up that hot canyon a second time to look at them. There they are. The Indians made 'em. So what?" These marks

from an ancient world continuing right into the present
held no wonder for Buzz.

If Whit had not talked a good deal about the pre-
historic tribes of Dinosaur they might have had little
meaning for the rest of them. But over the years Whit
had absorbed a fair amount of Indian lore. He had
voted for a trip on the Yampa, instead of on the Green
River, because there some of the Indian caves had been
dug out by archeologists. But white water won the day
and Whit had to content himself with these few paintings done in red ocher on a slab of rock.

"They're childish paintings," Whit explained, "because the men who did them in five or six hundred
A.D. were childish people. Lazy people too, as far as
anyone can find out. They had a nice little paradise
here—plenty of fish and game, wood for their fires, and
valleys which stayed warm all winter where they could
grow corn. No reason to work hard. Nobody knows how
long those early tribes lasted, or where they went. The
Utes, who came much later, were a different race al-
together."

By the time she reached these relics Andy had built
up a real sense of awe over the idea of looking at anything so old. Everyone with a camera photographed
the crook-horned creature which seemed to be a mountain sheep and the human figure in a feathered head-
dress which Whit said probably represented a chief.

Everyone, that is, took pictures of the rock paintings
except Lance. On the top of a pine tree he spotted a
lazuli bunting, "blue as the bluest summer sky" he
called it afterward, and by the time he followed his
bird across the creek, up the mountainside and down
again, he was halfway back to camp. He never did see
the pictographs.

If the Indian paintings were disappointing to Buzz,
the fishing was even more so. "I warned you," Ollie

told him. "Flash flood last year took out about every fish in Jones Crick."

"Then where'd you get those?" Buzz demanded, eying the eight trout Ollie was cleaning.

Ollie's face puckered into accordion pleats until his eyes looked like little bright holes. "Me? Oh, I just sweet-talk the fish, Buzz. And they come jumpin' right into my creel."

Buzz grunted and went off to deal with his one small trophy.

One thing which Ollie had not promised at Jones Creek turned out to be for Andy the greatest fun of all. The river was wider and shallower here than in the upper part of the canyon, the current just swift enough to carry one person downstream on an inflated air mattress.

"Mattress sailing," Johan Speiser named it, as, enchanted with this unadvertised American sport, he let himself float down the river and walked back upstream to coast down over again during most of the hot lazy afternoon. At first Johan, like the others, lay flat on his mattress, paddling with both hands to steer. Presently he tried sitting up and finally standing. This last toppled him promptly into the water, where he found the rocks too close for comfort. "What do you think you're riding, a surfboard?" Lance teased.

Sometimes Andy, Lance, and Johan took the riffles three abreast, Lance holding her hand on one side of the mattress, Johan on the other. They all felt gay and silly and laughed at each other, or at nothing at all, until their feet were sore from trudging over the round river stones. Then the three of them stretched out on the beach to rest, replenishing their energy with Johan's supply of Swiss chocolate and listening spellbound to his tales of German rivers and German ways.

"Are you married, Johan?" Lance asked, after hearing him describe a particularly hair-raising episode.

The brown hands gestured thumbs down. "Me? I am married to my foldboat. What wife would like to stay home and think about her husband spinning on his head in a nice whirlpool?"

"A wife might enjoy foldboating too," Andy put in quickly.

"Ah—there speaks the true American girl. But American or not, it is a subject to which you should give some thinking, Miss Andy." Johan sat up to flick a box-elder bug from the back of his neck, remained that way, looking down into Andy's face as if he were studying her.

"You someday may be a champion of the foldboats. Already you have great skill for one so young. You have also—how do I say it in English?—much put-to-gether-ness."

"Co-ordination is the word you're reaching for—I think," Lance told him. "Andy certainly has a lot of it."

"Co-ordination. Exactly. The brain, the hand, the arm, the body balance—all at one time. But you have more, Andy. You work. You have passion to win—even a mattress sailing race," he finished, laughing.

Leaning comfortably against the sandy bank, Andy felt too relaxed, too happy in the pinpoint of the moment to consider Johan's advice very seriously. "I'll remember," she told him dreamily—"when the time comes. I'll refuse to marry any man who objects to my spinning on my head in a nice whirlpool."

Johan let his superbly muscled body fall back again, lay staring up through the sun-spattered branches. "To marry is to have a house," he said thoughtfully. "For me, if I can choose, forever I would live under the sky with no roof at all. Perhaps then I learn some of the things your American Indians knew so well."

"Like what?" Andy wanted to know.

"Oh—to know like brothers all the small creatures of the forest. To say, 'This way a band of wild sheep has passed.' To smell the rain before it comes. Air of the city is death to the nose."

"I like thinking about the Indians who lived in this canyon before us," Lance said. "And the trappers who came after them. And the explorers like Powell. We aren't here for any important reason as they were but knowing that they traveled this way too seems to make us all one big family of—"

Bouncing upright again, Johan interrupted. "But we are here for a reason. Important reason too. Cities—they kill something in a man. Make him a puppet pulled by strings. On the river I find my soul. Now you can laugh at this sentimental German."

But they did not laugh. Both Lance and Andy felt his meaning. Later, when Johan had gone to dress, Lance said, "This week has been much too short, Andy. Here it is almost our last day and I've barely begun to know Johan Speiser. He's far from being just an athlete."

Andy nodded, wondering for a moment if the last phrase was aimed at her. But the golden light filtering through the leaves was reflected in her warm brown eyes as she answered teasingly, "I'm glad you started talking to me on the very first day. By now I know *you* are much more than just a photographer." It was a great deal for Andy to express to a boy.

On that last evening at Jones Hole, Andy did not need to look at Ollie in white chef's cap and apron to feel festive. Nor at the green boughs which decorated the smoking lamb as Ollie unwrapped it from layers of cloth in which it had baked all day under hot stones. As Ollie brandished his carving knife steam rose from the roast and went spiraling up through the trees with

hunger-making fragrance. He cut into it. Juice ran.
Mouths watered. Cheers rose. And Andy moved on
wings.

Buzz faded from her thoughts. Even the solid fact
that in a few days Lance would be in Oregon, where
she might never see him again, was pushed into some
dim corner of her mind. Now was the perfect time.
The future could take care of itself. Tonight they were
friends.

She felt easy, happy—a trifle lightheaded perhaps—
but more completely herself than she remembered ever
feeling in her life. She was not just one fifth of the
Dawson family, doing what she was told to do, or what
Dawsons were supposed to do. She was Andrea—separate—out on her own.

At the end of campfire Chuck gave his usual preview
of the next day's run on the river. "The first thing we
strike is Whirlpool Canyon. Not as bad as it sounds.
Then the river slows down, widens out, and wanders
all over the map to get around Island Park. At Rainbow
Park we'll eat lunch and walk around a bit to get
strong for the afternoon dash through Split Mountain.
Split Mountain is a series of rapids. Tricky, but no big
drop-off like Hell's Half. Schoolboy Rapids comes first.
Ollie named that one because he said any schoolboy
could run it. You can argue the point with him later.
But the one to watch is Sob.

"At Rainbow Park, Johan will take the lead and
Ollie, as usual, will be rear guard in case anyone runs
into trouble. You won't, though. You're graduate River
Runners now, and I'm proud of every one of you.
That's all for tonight except that we're awarding a little
prize to the person we think shows the greatest im-
provement in boat handling since we left Brown's Park."

Chuck fished a package out of his hip pocket. It was
wrapped in crumpled tissue paper, tied with a piece of

fishline. "A committee of three, Ollie, Whit, and yours truly, picked the winner after a lot of very serious thought—and considerable competition. These four magnificent chocolate bars now go to Timothy Frayne." When the hand clapping subsided Chuck went on. "At the start of this trip these big old cliffs sort of got Tim down. But if any of you have paddled along behind him during the last few days you'll agree with the committee that he has the makings of a great foldboater. Come get your prize, Tim."

Looking startled as a young buck surprised in the forest, Tim squared his shoulders and walked forward to take the candy from Chuck. Across the fire Andy saw Martha flick the back of a hand against the corners of her eyes.

Chuck's done it again, Andy thought. He's dreamed this up especially to give Tim the boost he needs. *Sotto voce* she said to Lance, "That Chuck—he sees right down inside of people—and then does something about it."

"He's quite a guy," Lance said under his breath. "When I first saw him on Ollie's lawn in shorts, all knobby knees and elbows, raking those four hairs on the top of his head the way he does when he's thinking hard, I couldn't figure why *he* was your leader. But I certainly know now."

"It was Chuck who started me foldboating," Andy said fondly. "Now it means more to me than anything in the world."

The evening was over, but no one wanted to leave the fire. It was not for warmth they sat there, but because a fire under the open sky has a strange hypnotic pull. Buzz took out his harmonica and a few people sang softly, drifting through those old songs which carry on from generation to generation, cutting their

channels into human hearts as surely as the running
river cuts its channel into the earth.

"I suppose I should go along to bed," Andy said wistfully. "Split Mountain sounds as if it would need all
I have."

"Don't go yet. It's our last night out." Lance reor-
ganized his legs on more comfortable lines.

"I know. Our last campfire."

As if he were pulling them out of the coals into
which he was looking so intently, the words of a poem
he had once liked enough to learn came back to Lance.
He spoke them hesitantly.

> "Strange how men love to huddle by a blaze,
> A telltale mark of those ancestral days
> When fire stood between us and the maw
> Of sabre-tooth and the marauding claw,
> Barring the evil spirits of the night—

"I've forgotten the rest."

"A poet as well as a photographer," Andrea said, so
quietly she might have been speaking to herself.

There were no real good nights that evening. One by
one people wandered off to bed, their flashlights show-
ing like fireflies among the trees. Lance and Andrea sat
until Ollie stood over the embers with a bucket of
water. "Time to hit the sack, kids," he told them.
"You've got work to do tomorrow."

CHAPTER ELEVEN

The feeling of lightheaded joy which had surged through Andrea during the two days at Jones Hole was still with her when she wakened the next morning. Even the little red box-elder bugs which crowded the undersides of the leaves all night, only to come crawling into her sleeping bag at first light, tickling as they walked, failed to annoy her. There were a few clouds moving about in the sky, covering and uncovering the sun. But that did not matter either. Let it rain. It would be a warm rain. Today nothing could quell her deep inner happiness.

She had squeezed the last bit of air out of her mattress, rolled the sleeping bag, and shoved them both into a dunnage with the rest of her belongings long before Finette and Martha were packed. Hoisting the bag onto one shoulder, she walked with springy strides down to the beach. The thrill which came each morning when she saw her own boat waiting on the bank had not diminished. In fact, day by day the bright blue canvas streak grew to be more a part of her being. Andrea and the boat were one. It was a passport to fresh worlds, and when the low-voiced boom of plunging water sounded ahead, heralding the moment when the current would seize the two of them—that was heaven. That was what she lived for.

Finette joined Andy presently, lugging her own bag and waving a belt, a scarf, and a piece of Andy's underwear. Finette's face sparkled with mischief. "Seems to me you were in a mighty big hurry this morning, Andy. Are you that eager to shuffle off your old bunkie on the last day?"

"Aw—Finette!" Andy wrapped both arms around Finette's neck. "You know I'm not. I'll miss you madly. It's been perfect camping with you—sleeping right alongside, talking. I wish it could go on forever. It's much more fun than rooming with my sister."

Finette still looked amused. "Don't you like your sister?"

"Of course I like her. Marianne's a darling. It's just that—oh, I can't explain. Perhaps it's simply that she *is* my sister. She makes me feel like a little girl and you don't, even though you're older than Marianne."

"You know what, Andy?" Finette stepped back to inspect the girl who faced her, vivid as a garden of spring flowers. "I think," she said slowly, "that you are too excited to be entirely sane. And I don't believe river running has a thing to do with it."

Instantly Andy became wrapped in dignity. "How silly can you get?" she asked, trying hard to sound casual, and began wedging the clothes Finette had picked up into her bag.

Andy took the life preserver out of her boat and strapped it on. She really wanted to get down inside for a look at the adhesive cast she had put on the cracked longeron. But by now there were too many people on the beach. Someone would be sure to say, "What's the matter? Lose something?" And peer in to help find it. So she contented herself with reaching under the deck to feel the patch job. The tape seemed

just as smooth as when she had first applied it. She put
the boat in the water, stepped in and let it drift toward the riffles where she had gone mattress sailing so
gaily with Lance and Johan.

The boat handled as well as ever. The extra layers
seemed to have no effect on guiding or balance, and
suffused as she was with rosy happiness, Andy let the
whole matter slide out of her mind.

Monk and Liz were next to put in. They passed her
with their usual cheery "Hi! How's everything?"

"Couldn't be better," Andy sang back. She watched
their nicely synchronized paddling until Monk's carrottop vanished around a bend in the river.

Still she paddled lazily through quiet water. I'm
never going to be like Johan, Andy told herself, married to my foldboat. No matter how good I get to be.
Liz and Monk have the answer to that one. It did not
occur to her that it was Liz who had fitted herself into
Monk's plan of life rather than the other way around.

Something Chuck had said long ago—oh, years back
when she first began sharing his boat—came to mind
now. Andy had complained to him, "I have to think so
hard all the time I'm paddling. It wears me down."

"You won't always have to," Chuck had told her.
"Someday you can just lean against your back rest and
ride along as easily as you walk. And when that time
comes you'll be good." The time had now come.

The entire morning went by like a dream, a timeless
moment of beauty. This new unstated gladness made
the river itself look different. Patterns of foam on the
surface of the water, leaves shimmering along the bank,
cloud shadow turning the rocks deep blue and purple,
a whiff of sagebrush carried on the wind—never had
she been so intensely aware of these things. And all
the while pictures of Lance crowded her head. The
way he used his hands, his hair which he said had a

will of its own, the candid gray-green eyes. It was indeed a rapturous morning.

When a beaver plopped off the bank with a spank of
his tail and swam right in front of her, she called out
to him, "Morning, Beaver! How are you and all the
little beavers today?" Beaver did not answer. He merely
kept on swimming toward the opposite bank. Andrea
did not care. She sucked in a deep breath of air, sweet
with the scent of green growing things, and her mouth
curved into a smile.

After the swift descent through Whirlpool Canyon
the river changed its tempo. On its great loop around
Island Park it became a meandering stream with pastoral-looking banks.

At Rainbow Park they ate lunch under the trees, and
Andy walked about afterward with Lance to stretch
their legs. It was good to be alone together, yet neither one of them had much to say. Lance, too, seemed
to be moving in a dream. It was as if they were both
holding their breaths waiting for something to happen.

Mae Wests and spray covers were fastened on; Johan
led off with Chuck and Finette close behind. Even
when Connie went by with the fantastic haircut Buzz
had given him, Andy could whip up no rancor, "Que
sera sera," she thought. Buzz is the way he is, and
after today he will be out of my life forever.

She looked back, hoping to fix in her mind one of
those mental landscapes Lance had talked about. This
would be a painting of a place where she had eaten
lunch and been particularly happy. She saw Ollie wave
at his flock as he and Buzz and the two Van Fleets
pulled away from shore.

On this last run through Split Mountain, Andy
wanted to stay as close as possible to Johan. His paddling is so beautiful, she thought, and it's my last
chance to learn from watching him. It may be years

before I have another ride behind one of the champions of the world. No—she corrected herself. Not too many years. By the time I'm twenty-one I should be good enough to make a try at the Arkansas race. With an effort she pulled herself out of the trancelike state in which she had drifted all day and dug the paddle into the water to catch up.

"What's the big hurry, Andy?" Liz asked as she overtook them.

"Can't wait to see where Monk's friends, the dinosaurs, got buried," Andy sang back, and kept paddling as fast as she was able.

Schoolboy Rapids, which any schoolboy could take with one hand tied behind him, were another bit of Ollie's whimsy. The route lay between two bold rocks, a narrow gate, forcing the water into a torrent.

Johan kept to the center of the stream. Andy saw him rise up on his knees for an instant to get a better view of what he was approaching. Then he let the current carry him diagonally across the river toward the sluiceway between the rocks. By the time he reached it his narrow slalom boat was headed directly into the channel, took it cleanly, straight on. Johan shifted his balance and bobbed along over the rough water toward a chain of haystacks below.

It looked quite easy. Chuck and Finette went through the same maneuver, and Andy shot after them with a glow of satisfaction at being able to control her boat so accurately. When the river became quieter she looked around for Lance. She had not seen him in some time and decided he was loitering to take a few last pictures.

Only one more real challenge lay ahead—several minor ones—but only Sob was truly treacherous. Andy sang exuberantly, "One more rapid, there's one more rapid to cross."

All her life she would treasure the memory of this
week on the river. It had been much more than a vacation, more than just another outing with the River
Runners. A different girl was coming out of the canyon
from the one who went in. The long hours of paddling
day after day had improved her technique, but it was
more than that. Johan said she had put-together-ness.
What he referred to was, of course, a physical thing.
But actually she felt an inner put-together-ness she had
never known before, as if in this one week she had
miraculously found out who she was and where she was
going.

Andy saw Chuck take off his hat and wave it in the
air. It was a signal she knew well. The distant drumming sound must be from Sob. Closer and closer it
came, louder and louder, throbbing between the two
stone walls which compressed its fury.

There was a clutch of excitement in her throat as
she licked her lips and gripped the paddle more firmly.
A few more seconds now and she would be water-
flying. Bracing her knees and feet to meet the oncoming
moment of stress, she watched the water. By now
much of what she had to do was instinctive, but it still
required a complete focus of attention. Guiding a foldboat was in many ways like driving an automobile. In a
car it was rarely safe to take your eyes from the road. In
a boat on swift water it was never safe to look away.

The ease with which Johan moved downstream fascinated her. She knew how much more difficult his boat
was to manage than her own, or any of the others, because once in still water she had asked him to let her
paddle about in it. She had nearly upset just climbing
in. But with his graceful, highly individual style he
took it through waves with the cool unconcern of a boy
on a bicycle, disdaining handle bars. The unconcern,
Andy knew, was pure illusion. Johan was careless about

nothing. He not only watched the river but saw details of movement which most people missed.

The rumble of rushing water became deafening. Then the current took her into its arms and swept her on a relentless course. Everywhere water lashed at the rocks.

Andrea strained forward, trying to see exactly how Johan was paddling. And in that second, as she lifted her eyes from the river, a cross current caught her bow and swung it viciously around. Thousands of pounds of water came battering against the side of the boat. It seemed as if the mountain itself were lunging at her. Desperately Andy drove the paddle into the water, trying to head the boat downstream again. But in that spot the strength of ten men could not have pulled it straight. She went careening along broadside, helpless as a drowning mouse in the thundering swirl of water. She tried to study the river as she churned through it. If she could stay right side up for another twenty yards there was a quieter-looking pool ahead where her strength might be enough to swing the bow downstream again.

"Save your energy till your chance comes," she ordered sternly. "Don't panic. Concentrate! Concentrate on not getting swamped. With a horrible grinding the bottom of the boat scraped over a submerged rock. For a moment it teetered wildly. Then the avalanche of water wrenched it away and whipped it against another boulder jutting through the spume. The sickening crack of splintered wood rose above the crash of the rapids. The whole boat shivered. It seemed to rise up in the middle until it bent in half. Andy felt the rush of water against her legs. With agony she knew what had happened. This was disaster. Total disaster.

CHAPTER TWELVE

Andrea never reached the quiet pool twenty yards downstream. Like a twig in a torrent, the water took her, battering her back and forth as she tried to defend herself from the bruising granite. One hand still clutched the paddle. Then the top caught under a snag, and she was torn away from it. Water blinded her. Water was in her mouth and ears. She felt herself being rolled over and over, bounced about as if by some gigantic malevolent hand.

I'm bound to stay up, she thought. The Mae West won't let me sink. The Mae West will save me from the rocks. Again she spun helplessly in the maelstrom. Look out for your head, look out for your head. . . . that was the last thing Andy remembered. The rest Johan told her as she lay coughing and spitting on a narrow shelf of rock at the edge of the river.

"The first I see is half a blue boat flying past me, crazy in the rapids. I seem to know for sure it is your boat. I look behind. There is no other half. There is no girl with yellow hair. Then I see the Mae West rolling in the foam. I shout to Chuck. He sees too, but with Finette in the boat he is helpless. A man may place his own life in danger, but not that of another. For

truth we are both helpless. The water is too mad to
stop. But I think perhaps I can delay. I back-paddle
to slow down—is no good.

"Then I see coming a big rock. Please, rock, I say,
have for me a little quiet place of water on this side.
I think to make an eddy anchor against the rock while
the current goes by on each side. The eddy is there—
but to get into it in a slalom is not easy. So I shout to
you, 'Grab the float balls.' But your hand does not move
and your face does not smile at me. Then I know I
must catch you somehow by the shirt or by the hair
as you go by. A little prayer comes to me, Andy, for you.
For me too—for strength to get into the eddy, for strength
to hold you until we find a place to land.'"

Andy scarcely seemed to hear the story Johan was
pouring out. Passionately she sobbed, "My boat! It's
gone! Gone!"

"But *you* are here, Andy. We are so lucky." Rhyth-
mically Johan rubbed his powerful hands over her back
and neck.

Shaking from head to foot, Andy continued to sob.
Her teeth chattered.

Johan picked up one of her arms, then the other,
chafed them roughly to bring the blood back into cir-
culation. Nothing seemed to stop the shivering of her
body. Her boat was smashed. Useless. And with it the
whole bright edifice of confidence and happiness which
Andy had built up during the past week crashed to the
ground—a mess of broken shards. She had made a fool
of herself, an utter fool. She was not worth her father's
trust, or all Chuck's help. She was a no-good foldboater.
Champion! The word burst bitterly from her mouth as
again she broke into gusts of sobbing that racked her
from head to foot.

Johan caught only the word champion, thought she
was speaking to him, complimenting him on his rescue.

"But it was nothing, Andy. What anybody would have done. We had great good luck to find before it is too late this little seat of rock where I can get you out of the water. At first you seem unconscious. Your head, I tell myself, has hit a rock. Then I realize you are only full of shock and—what you call it?—not thinking well —dizzy from the tossing by the river."

Andy could not answer him. She had stopped coughing and sputtering; she did not hurt physically. But within she felt crushed.

"Better for you that you sit up now," Johan said. "In a minute Ollie will be here. I see them now above. I am not sure they can stop here where we are. The current is too strong for them, I think. With the foldboat it was most difficult to land. We must think, Andy, think how we get out of this place we sit in." As gently as if she had been a baby Johan turned her over onto her back, made her sit propped against his shoulder. "So! Better, is it not?"

"Oh, Jo-h-han. You're too good—t-to me," Andy stuttered between still chattering teeth.

"Please, Andy. Do not try to talk." Johan continued rubbing her hands and arms. "For the first time in your life you have felt the terrible power of running water. Is a thing to shake the soul of a person older than you. But now is time to stop crying. You must *act* brave—as you *are*."

"Don't praise me." Andy bent her head in shame. "I was stupid—stupid!"

Johan did not argue the point. "Now," he said, "look up the river. Here is Ollie and that big Buzz to help us."

The cumbersome raft edged close to the rock where Andy and Johan were huddled. Andy did not lift her head from her chest. She could not bear the thought of facing anyone. Buzz will be laughing, she thought. He'll be laughing himself sick because now I've had it.

Ollie's command to Buzz rang above the clamor of the water. "Hold her close as long as you can. Hard, boy! *Harder*. Put your back into it." Rowing with all his power against the thrust of the river, Ollie bellowed, "Can't stop here. We'll beach her just below. Crawl up behind you with a rope." The raft was swept past them.

Johan got to his feet, pulling Andrea up after him. "If you could move a little bit, Andy, jump up and down, beat your hands together. That would help you, I think."

For the first time since she had come out of the water, Andy looked about her. It was indeed a narrow bench of rock on which they were huddled. It sloped sharply to the river, the lower edge so close to water level that it lay constantly wet and slippery with spray. When they both sat down, there was no space for Johan's boat. He had dragged the bow up onto the ledge, fastening the tie rope around a small outcrop of rock. But most of the boat bobbed recklessly in the turbulent chop.

It was the danger to Johan's beautiful racer that brought Andy to her senses. "Your boat," she cried. "Don't leave it there. It keeps bumping against the rocks. It will be ruined."

"Better boat than girl," Johan said. "Here where we are is not much room."

"But you can't leave it that way. Look! If we both stand smack up against this wall behind us, we can get the whole boat onto the ledge." Impulsively she moved toward the bow of his boat.

Johan grabbed her arm. "Careful, Andy. Under our feet is like glass. And you still shaky."

"But your beautiful boat!" Boat, boat. It was an obsession in her brain.

Johan caught her by both arms. This time he spoke sternly. "Leave the boat alone. I forbid you to touch it. If you are able to wait quietly for a few minutes, I will pull it out of the water. At least most of it. Then we must both stand with our backs to this rock until help comes. You feel strong enough now to stand?"

Andy nodded. He pushed her flat against the stone. "There. Do not stir. One careless step and quite easily we could both slide into the river."

He untied the boat, hauling it up onto the bench as step by step he moved backward until he stood beside Andy. With one hand he grasped her arm, with the other he held the rope of his boat.

The time of waiting seemed to stretch on and on. There were moments when Andy thought her knees were going to buckle so that she would collapse on top of the boat, skidding all of them back into the water. Then with infinite effort she pulled herself erect and tried to breathe evenly and slowly.

Johan talked to her quietly. "You must not chastise yourself, Andy, or call yourself stupid because you have lost a boat. This can happen to all. You will have another boat and go out on the water again as soon as is for you possible. Like the fliers of airplanes, you dare not let the fear from one accident have time to grow solid in your mind."

"I'll never have another boat. I wouldn't think of asking for one," Andy said, all the sweetness of her wide red mouth pulled to a tight line. "Why should I beg my father to give me another when I lost this by my own stupidity? I'm no good, I tell you. I'm a lousy fold-boater. Plain lousy." The shivering of her body had stopped, but her breath still came in jerks as gusts of remorse swept her.

"But I do not understand. Why do you call yourself stupid? This is not easy—this Green River."

"Don't—d-don't make me explain. But I was. I know —and I was." The words were passionate, spoken from the depths of Andrea's being. "I don't deserve another boat and I'm not worthy of all the work Chuck wasted on me."

In her own mind Andrea was not entirely clear about the reason for her disaster. The whole thing had happened so fast she could not separate the strands which led up to it. Had she been so intent on watching Johan that she was careless? Or had the cracked longeron given way, sending the boat out of control? The guilt of this last was a searing thing. She should have reported it to Chuck at once, letting him decide whether it was safe. If it had not been for all the incidents with Buzz she might have done so. Though in her heart she knew what a wrench it would have been to give up paddling down the river with Lance. As it was, she had been foolhardy, cocky, the complete show-off, sure nothing could happen to her.

Johan did not question her further. He stood close, giving her as much physical support as possible by making her lean against him.

After a long wait they heard a voice from the top of the rock at their backs. Looking up, carefully so her still unsteady feet would not slip, Andy saw Buzz standing about twenty feet above her head with a rope in his hand.

"Listen, Jo. Ollie wants to know if I pull Andy up on the rope, can you launch your boat from here? Or do we pull you and the boat up too?"

Cupping his hands to make his voice carry, Johan shouted back. "Myself, I make it down the river. Can you take Andy?"

For answer Buzz lowered the rope with an old quilt tied to its end. "Ollie says to wrap her in the quilt so she won't get scraped."

"Is Ollie with you?" Johan wanted to know.

"Sure. Pretty close. The footing's not too good right where I'm standing. Ollie's back of me, holding the rope wrapped around a bush."

Johan folded the comforter about Andy's body, fastened the rope into a sling and signaled that they were ready. Buzz sat down on the edge of the rock, letting his huge feet hang over the edge. Very slowly he began to pull on the rope, while Ollie took up the slack. Part way up Andy felt herself jerk to a stop. The quilt was caught on a jag of rock. Buzz yanked at it until the cloth ripped apart and she moved upward once more, as inch by inch he fed the rope through his huge hands. When he had her level with his own feet, Buzz stopped hauling and grinned down into Andy's face.

"So Miss Spitfire got hers," he said. "Old Buzz, the boatman, wasn't high-toned enough for you. You had to go making time with a bird chaser. But you'll be mighty glad to have my arms around you now." He finished pulling her up and sat cradling her as if she had been a baby.

"Put me down," Andy said furiously. This was more than her jolted nerves could take. Buzz was having the last laugh all right, and he was squeezing the last drop of pleasure from it.

With Andy still in his arms Buzz stood up and jumped across a narrow crack between the rocks.

"Put me down, I tell you. Let me out of this harness. I can walk." Andy was screaming at him.

"Not right here you can't," Buzz said.

"Where's Ollie?" she demanded.

"Right there. Open your eyes and look, you little hellcat you."

Ollie came toward them quickly. His ropewise fingers unfastened the sling. "Tough luck, Andy," he said. "You feel all right? Think you can walk back to the raft?

It's not far, only the going is rough as all get out. Not dizzy, are you? Or sick to your stomach?"

Andy shook herself free of the quilt contaminated by Buzz's touch. "I'm perfectly all right. Just jittery, I guess. Stay near me, Ollie. My legs feel like rubber."

"Let me carry you down, Andy. I can do it easily." Once more Buzz started to pick her off the ground.

But Ollie stopped him. "Let her walk—if she can. Walking is good for whatever ails you except a broken leg."

Stumbling often, Andy picked her way across the broken rock. It was hard work, and more than once she reached for Ollie's hand to hold her balance. But in spite of an upriver wind blowing against her wet clothes, she had stopped shivering. Ollie was right—walking is good for whatever ails you. Her body was beginning to recover from the tumbling the river had given it. But the girl—Andrea—the essence within—remained a pulp of broken pride.

Two foldboats were waiting beside the raft. As Andy approached, Finette dashed up to throw both arms around her. "Darling! You're safe! Oh, Andy, I love you so much."

"Don't, Finette. Please. Don't sympathize with me or I'll burst out crying again. And I *won't* give Buzz that much satisfaction."

Chuck and Lance walked with her to the raft, one on each side. "What happened, Andy? You were going great guns all morning." Chuck's boring eyes made her wince.

Andy shrugged. She couldn't talk about it now. In fact she was never going to talk about foldboating again. What was the use? She had failed inexcusably. Clearly she did not have the stuff in her that champions are made of.

Ollie laid his own bedding roll on top of the food boxes in the center of the raft, arranging it so that she could recline facing forward. He wrapped the torn comforter around her legs and came back again with a tin cup which he held to her lips.

"Here. Drink this."

Andy wrinkled her nose at the smell. "What is it?"

"Drink it. It's good for you." Somewhere inside of Ollie there was steel. Good-natured, easygoing, relaxed as an old shoe while he went about his routine tasks; when Ollie gave commands, like those he gave Buzz on how to handle the oars, you obeyed without argument.

Andy swallowed. The brandy burned her throat and made her eyes water, but presently, as the raft pushed out into midstream, a warm sense of relaxation stole through her. She wished she could go to sleep right there and not wake up again until she was home. At the end of Split Mountain Canyon the others would be waiting, full of questions, full of talk. "What happened? Did you snag your paddle? Did a rock jump right up out of the water and hit you? She could almost guess the comment that would come from each one, excited, tender, joking, or plain curious. No one would be unsympathetic, no one would gloat as Buzz was doing over her downfall. Nevertheless, she longed to burrow into the ground where she could hide from every person who reminded her of what she had done—and of what she had hoped to do.

The chatter was not long in coming. Mrs. Van Fleet left her husband's side and edged forward until she was within talking distance of Andrea. "I think this river running is perfectly terrible. I've known all along somebody was going to get hurt. You poor child, it's a wonder you weren't killed."

"Well, I wasn't." Andy wanted to add, "Are you disappointed?" but bit back the rudeness. She closed her eyes, hoping Mrs. Van Fleet would think she had dozed off, or passed out from Ollie's brandy.

But Mrs. Van Fleet was not an easy talker to deter. "Does the glare hurt your eyes? Here, take my hat." Forcibly she lifted Andy's head and put her own hat on top of it.

Andy promptly handed it back again. "There isn't any glare. The clouds have almost covered the sun. I'm just tired. It was sort of a hard swim."

"Hard swim! As if anybody could swim a stroke in this frightful torrent. I simply can't understand what makes people want to go through rapids in little tiny boats. Even in this big thing I'm scared to death every time we hit a bumpy place."

Poor Connie, Andy thought. No wonder he wants to get away from home every weekend. A deep sense of thankfulness for her own parents, so long taken for granted, had been slowly growing inside of Andrea as she watched Connie with his mother.

The flat voice rattled on. "I tell you, if Connie was not twenty-one years old I'd put my foot down on this foldboat business. There must be other ways for a young man to enjoy himself without risking his neck every week."

Now, Andy thought, now's the time to put in a word for Connie. "But people have to go away from home, Mrs. Van Fleet. To grow up, they have to."

"Well, not from our home. Why, Papa and I would just love to have Conrad bring his friends to the house oftener. We'd do our best to give them a good time, and I know we set a lovely table. But all he seems to want to do is go off with you people every minute he can spare from his schoolwork."

"You ought to give a good party for Connie while he

still has his Green River haircut," Buzz told her. "That
would sure make him famous."

Mrs. Van Fleet sniffed.

Andy cast about for something pleasant to think of,
anything which would make her numb to the voice
at her side. Still it went on and on, insistent as a buzzing
mosquito in the early morning. You could slap at it, but
the next minute the whine would begin again at your
other ear.

While the raft carried her down through the last rugged gorge of the dinosaur country Andy did not lift
her head or open her eyes to look at the cliffs she had
loved so much. Not until she heard the crunch of gravel
on the bottom and felt a slight bump did she sit up.
Buzz had shipped his oars and was already on the
beach, hauling at the rope to pull them ashore.

Clouds covered the sun completely now and under
their shadow the river looked black. The canyon was
gone. The barricade of Split Mountain shut off all view
of the tumbling river down which they had floated for
so many lovely days. Standing on this arid plain for the
first time, a stranger would never guess all that lay behind the narrow slit in that stone slab. Here on the
western side of Split Mountain was only desert, tree-
less and bleak, broken by low eroded hills.

A dozen hands reached to help Andy climb out of the
raft. She took one of them blindly. Then, on the beach
among the other boats, most of them already knocked
down for packing, she saw the two sagging halves of
her own.

CHAPTER THIRTEEN

Martha was the first to grasp from Andy's drained face that something more had happened to her than the loss of a boat. She tried to shepherd her into the bus as quickly as possible, hoping to guard her from the sympathy as well as the questions of the other River Runners.

But Andy would not go. She walked to her boat, bent over the mangled frame, fingering the collapsed deck. Was it only a month ago she had set it up so proudly on the living-room floor? The whole scene came flooding back, every part of it a searing hurt. Her father, sprawled in the big chair by the window, the smell of his pipe, Marianne's fingers, red-tipped on the white piano keys, and herself sitting inside the boat with all the pride and hope and excitement that boiled in her that day. How could she face them again? How go back and explain that this bright blue treasure was kindling wood, not worth bringing home?

And they would want to know every detail of how it came to happen. That, too, was a tangled web. Was she daydreaming about Lance as she had been most of the day? Was she watching Johan instead of the river? Or had the cracked longeron given away completely, sending the boat out of control? None of these things was easy to explain to a family. Worst of all, she herself was not really sure which one had caused the wreck. She might never know. Possibly it was all three.

"Chuck carried half your boat in," Martha said matter-of-factly. "Or what used to be half. Lance found the front end piled up on a rock and brought it along, thinking there might be some salvage value in the hull. The experts all agree the boat itself can't possibly be repaired."

"No, it can't," Andy said tonelessly. "I can see that. And I don't want the hull." She reached down to snap off a bit of wood from one splintered rib, studied it in her open palm for a moment, then shoved it into the pocket of her jeans. "All right. Let's get into the bus. I wish we were going straight back to Vernal. The last thing I want to do is look at dinosaur fossils. I feel dead and buried myself."

But for everyone except Andrea the quarry, where masses of Mesozoic bones had been discovered, and the museum beside it were an excitement not to be missed. It was these ancient bones, and not the wild beauty of the rivers, which first led Woodrow Wilson to set the area aside as a National Monument. The river country was added thirty years later. When digging began, dinosaur skeletons were carted away to eastern museums as fast as they could be uncovered. But many still remained, half exposed in the sandstone and carefully guarded now, so that Americans might better understand the land of which they were today the stewards.

Andy fell into a seat inside the bus and leaned her head against the dirty windowpane. Martha sat beside her. Neither spoke. When boats and baggage and people were finally loaded, Ollie's partner, who had driven to meet them here at Monument headquarters, gunned the motor and the wheezy old conveyance began grinding its way uphill to the museum.

What Andy really wanted was to stay inside the bus while the others wandered through the exhibits. But on second thought she decided it would be less conspicuous to go with them. Her one desire was to hide, to find a good big hole and jump into it. Questions and laughter and sympathy she dreaded equally.

Her conscience berated her because she had not reported the longeron break to Chuck. Perhaps this disaster was a just punishment for such deceit. And bitter medicine it had turned out to be.

All the way down the river Buzz had been secretly laughing at her. Right through Mrs. Van Fleet's steady trickle of chatter she could feel it. His mocking face said plainly, "Sister, you had this coming. And am I glad. You thought you were pretty smart getting your boy friend to jujitsu me into the river. And look what happened to you! Haw-haw-haw." Both as a foldboater and as a girl, she had failed miserably.

Lance liked her because she could do the things he liked to do, as Don had once liked her because she was a good skier. When skiing was out, Don dropped her like a hot potato. Now Lance—she pushed the picture of his face and all her thinking about him down inside herself as she had once put thoughts of Don into moth balls.

Trudging from glass case to glass case inside the museum, clinging to Martha's arm, Andrea looked but did not see.

She heard Timmie's voice on the other side of Martha. "Hey, Mom! There's a dinosaur no bigger than a chicken. The sign says it's full-grown too. I thought dinosaurs were all enormous."

"That's what most people think, Tim. But apparently they come in assorted sizes."

Tim was agog. "Come on, Mom. Let's get going. I want to see the quarry where the bones are lying right in the rock, the way they found them. Chuck was telling me about it the other day. All this country was swamp then, hot and steamy, like where crocodiles and alligators live now. They're the descendants of one family of dinosaurs, Chuck says. Shall we go, Mom?" He tugged gently at her arm.

"You go, Tim. I'll stay with Andy for a while."

"Go with him, Martha. I'm going back to the bus. I guess that rolling in the river took more out of me than I realized. I feel as if I'd been chewed up and spit out." She tried to conjure up a smile, failed miserably. Reluctantly Martha went with her son.

Andy climbed the rickety steps into the bus, chose a seat as far as possible from the man behind the wheel.

As she came in he turned to look. "You got sense," he said. "If ever I saw a bunch of overrated junk it's them old carcasses. People ooh and ah over them like they was looking at their first grandchild."

Yesterday Andy might have laughed. She might even have tried to convince the man, as Chuck would doubtless have done, that knowing what was on the earth eons ago made today easier to understand. Now her one desire was to be left alone. With her head on one arm, she curled up on the seat and pretended to sleep.

"Andy." It was Chuck's voice. Andrea felt her stomach tighten. He repeated her name a little louder. "Andy!" She opened her eyes.

"I hate to waken you. You've really had it today. But I wanted to talk to you alone for a minute and thought this might be our last chance."

Andy sat up to make room for him on the seat. Now it's coming, she thought. He's found the tape job in my boat. Aloud she said, "I know. You're leaving for Detroit right away."

"I won't even try to tell you, Andy, how sorry I am you cracked up. I know pretty well what that boat meant to you. But I have a hunch something more than the boat is bothering you, and I thought you might like to talk about it before I go."

Andy sat silently, twisting her fingers in her lap, wondering what to say.

"When did you put the adhesive on your central longeron?"

"You found it?"

"Lance discovered it first." Andy winced. "It was on the half he brought in. We examined it together. When did you put the tape on?"

"At Rippling Brook."

Chuck nodded. "That's what I figured. That rock in Hell's Half." In a voice half hurt, half puzzled, he went on. "Why didn't you let me have a look at it first?"

The square hands on Andrea's lap clasped so tightly, the nails whitened at their tips. Lance had promised Buzz not to tell Chuck about the rock rolling. Well, Andrea Dawson was not going to be the one to tattle. Anyhow, her aversion to riding on the raft was only a part of the story. The rest she scarcely understood herself. Perhaps it went way back to Don. Lance thought she was good on the river and above all else she wanted him to go on thinking so. She wanted to take her fold-boat right through to the end. How could she say these things to Chuck?

With bent head she said, "It's hard to explain, Chuck. It's all mixed up with Buzz and Lance and a lot of other stuff. It would take me the rest of the day to tell you."

Chuck gave a baffled sigh. "Buzz and Lance had some kind of a fight at Rippling Brook. That I know. And apparently Lance dunked Buzz in the river— which I'm sure he deserved—though how a string bean like Lance could outwrestle that moose is a major mystery to me."

"You don't miss many tricks, do you?" Andy said, smiling in spite of herself.

"Apparently I missed a very important one when you started off in a cracked boat, though fortunately——"

"It wasn't much of a break, Chuck, hardly big enough to get my fingernail into and I thought if I told you—I mean—well, I was afraid you'd make me ride the rest of the way in on the raft with Buzz and I couldn't possibly do that because——" Suddenly Andy hid her face on Chuck's shoulder. Once started, the dammed-up words poured from her in a waterfall.

"Oh, Chuck, I'm so miserable. And so ashamed. I wish I were dead. I wish I'd been killed in the rapids. That would have been easy. Now I have to go home and explain to my father and my mother and everybody will say, 'I told you so,' and it's the end of foldboating for me. I don't deserve another chance."

Up in the front seat the driver looked around to see what was going on. All he saw was a mop of yellow hair burrowing into the shoulder of a little man who fiddled with the top of his head.

"Andy, stop it! You're punishing yourself more than makes sense. And I don't know how the conversation got off on this track anyhow. I came in here to try to relieve your mind, not to scold you, or to pry into what went on between you and Buzz or you and Lance. That's your affair—strictly. But I did know you'd be feeling kind of upset because you didn't report a damaged boat. And I wanted to tell you that whatever it was caused your accident, it was *not* the cracked brace."

Andy lifted her head to stare at Chuck through blurry eyes. "You mean—you mean——?"

"I mean that the strongest piece of wood in your boat

seems to have been the one you wrapped up in tape. It was the only part that came through undamaged. Suffering cats! You must have used up a whole roll of adhesive. Don't you know that yellow stuff costs money?"

Andy felt too dazed to smile at Chuck's humor. "Then the reason I cracked up was just because I'm a lousy foldboater—not because I broke the rules."

"If you insist on looking at it that way—yes. But you're not a lousy foldboater—and you know it." Chuck sighed wearily. "I guess we all break safety rules once in a while, Andy. I certainly broke one the night I let you paddle Whit's boat from Angel Island to Point Richmond. Granted I didn't realize how difficult the trip was going to be until it was too late to do anything about it. But that's no excuse. Accidents are prevented by being fussy *before* they happen. That's why the River Runners have such a good record. We've lost boats—sure—but never a life. And please God, we never will."

Chuck let his intensity die down by looking out through the window on the opposite side of the bus. Tim Frayne was walking down the road with Connie Van Fleet, both of them laughing hilariously. In a more casual voice Chuck went on. "Personally I care too much about foldboating as a sport to take many chances. Think of the people it opens good new worlds for. I don't want anybody to pick up a paper and read about me in a river wreck and say, 'Those lunatics. They can have it.' It's fairly new in America, but I think it's something pretty fine. At least as good as skiing."

Chuck's voice was steadying. His gentleness was steadying. "It's better than skiing," Andy said shakily. "But don't worry, Chuck. This is the last time foldboating will ever get a bad press from me."

"You're not going to quit, Andy. That I *won't* have. Finette's ready for a boat of her own now and you can come back to paddling with me for a while. I've missed you. But you are *not* going to run out."

He gave her a pat on the back and stood up to leave. "Just thought you'd like to know the split wood was not responsible for your trouble. Don't make a habit of paddling around in a taped-up boat, though."

Only then, when impulsively she stretched out both hands to take both of his, did Andy notice that Chuck looked tired to death, gray even under his freckles. There were deep lines around his mouth and under his eyes the telltale crescents of fatigue.

"Forgive me, Chuck," she said. "Please."

"You're forgiven, Andy. We are all very grateful you didn't get hurt." Andrea had never heard Chuck speak so haltingly before. "Also very deeply in Johan's debt. Johan is probably one of two or three people in the whole world who could have pulled you out of that place—made such an impossible landing. Other men might have tried and gone down with you. As it was, Johan's own boat nearly got away. We are *all* lucky, my dear." He turned on his heel and dropped off the step of the bus to mingle with the dinosaur hunters.

CHAPTER FOURTEEN

The ride home, the long days with Lance, to which Andrea had looked forward so jubilantly, were now only another ordeal to be lived through. Being with Martha would not be hard. But Tim would ask questions, want a play-by-play account of the accident. Perhaps she could put him off with the story of Johan's skill and bravery and kindness. Oh, everyone had been so kind. Too kind. If they had beaten her up it might have been easier to take.

And Lance—what would he feel for her now? Contempt? Scorn for the show-off who thought that someday she was going to be a champion? What a laugh that turned out to be. Now she could go home and take up finger-painting again.

Martha was anxious to get back to San Francisco as soon as possible. So since Lance did not mind driving at night they left Vernal right after dinner. Lance and Martha rode on the front seat of Martha's hard-top; Tim sat in back with Andy. For the time being, that postponed talking to Lance, but Martha announced that after tonight they would take turns sitting in front. Lance drove fast, intent on the road, saying little. Tim went to sleep. It was late when they arrived at a motel

on the outskirts of Salt Lake City and checked in for
the night.

On that happy afternoon at Rippling Brook when
Finette lent her a green-checked shirt, Andy had kicked
herself for not packing a fresh cotton dress to wear
home. Tonight she couldn't have cared less. Standing
in her pajamas at the bureau of the motel room she
shared with Martha, Andy opened the top drawer to
put some of her draggled clothes out of sight. Inside
lay a black-bound book, a Bible, she supposed. She
opened it, looking for the psalm which begins, "I will
lift up mine eyes unto the hills, from whence cometh
my help." She loved that old pilgrimage psalm, sung
by the Israelites as they walked over their flat land,
raising hopeful eyes to a distant horizon. But when
she opened the book the words were totally strange.
Bewildered, she looked again at the title. She was holding the Book of Mormon, a solace no doubt to those
who had been brought up with it, but at that moment
it made Andy feel more than ever an outcast. She was
Ruth standing amid the alien corn. Shutting it away
once more inside the drawer, she fell into bed.

Early the next morning Martha wakened her. She
fished the other jeans from her dunnage bag and the
other faded shirt. They looked even grubbier indoors
than they had at Rippling Brook, but now it did not
seem to matter. Then with Martha she walked across
the court of the motel to breakfast. Lance and Tim
were already waiting for them outside the door of the
restaurant.

In spite of the brilliant sunlight on the street the
dining room was dim, the dark wooden booths lighted
by economical electric bulbs. The waitress showed them
to a booth for four and they slid in, Martha and Tim
on one side of the table, Andrea and Lance opposite.

At dinner in Vernal, Andy had wanted only a bowl

of soup and a glass of milk. The good-bys she still
had to say burdened her mind. Johan must be thanked
again. How did you thank a man adequately for saving
your life? "Thank you, Johan." The same words you
used when he passed the salt. Ollie and Buzz, dinner
guests of the River Runners that night, must also be
thanked. To thank Buzz seemed like groveling. Yet
common courtesy demanded it. However distasteful,
she was under an obligation to him for his share in her
rescue.

But this morning nature began reasserting herself.
Andy was ravenous. Martha was the one who settled
for coffee and toast, and Andy wondered if dollars made
the difference in their breakfast orders. This had been
an expensive holiday for Martha.

The waitress landed a sizzling platter on the table in
front of Andrea. The eggs were leathery on the bottom,
the potatoes greasy, and the bacon undercooked, but
Andy went at them hungrily. Suddenly she saw Martha
put down the toast she was nibbling and catch the edge
of the table with both hands, leaning forward to watch
something across the room. Seated opposite Martha, on
the inside of the high-walled booth, Andy could not
see what riveted her attention so completely.

Whatever it was, Tim was not interested. "Hot dog!"
he cried. "Real cow cream!" and emptied the pitcher
onto his oatmeal.

Andy laid down her own fork to stare at Martha.
Never before had she seen Martha look like that. Ten-
derness, pain, compassion, wonder? What was it? One
hand moved slowly toward her open mouth and, without taking her eyes from the thing which fascinated
her, the other hand reached across the table toward
Andy.

"Quick, Andy. I want you to change places with me.
There's something wonderful here in this dining room.

I want you to see it. I think it was meant for you to see."

"What on earth? You look so solemn. Can't I just look over the top of the booth?"

"No, no." Plainly Martha was excited. "Let her out, Lance. Hurry. I want you to sit right here where I am sitting."

The exchange of places was made quickly, a few plates and glasses pushed from one side of the table to the other, and Andy looked out across the dingy dining room.

A young woman in a wheel chair was being pushed toward a table by a tall young man. Behind them, on fat stubby legs, a baby boy marched alone. The child scrambled into a chair and rested his chin on the table, peering intently at his mother. Then began the business of transferring the young woman from the wheel chair to a seat at the table. Her husband—there was no question in Andy's mind that he was her husband—did not lift her. He did not even touch her arm. Bending above her head with hands poised to protect her against a slip, he watched her make the move entirely alone. Inch by inch, using her arms, she pulled herself into the new seat. It was a heroic effort. Both legs were obviously useless. But when finally she sat with both elbows resting on the table, she smiled at the two men in her family with such happiness that Andy understood why Martha had been transfixed.

By cover-girl standards it was not a beautiful face, but a unique radiance shone from it, an inner serenity, almost rapture. The tall young man folded the wheel chair and set it back against the wall out of sight. A waitress brought a high chair.

Andy looked over at Martha. "You mean 'There but for the grace of God go I'? Is that why you wanted me to trade seats with you?"

Reproachfully Martha shook her small sleek head

from side to side. "No, Andy. I just want you to look at that face and remember it—if you can. There is a happy woman."

"She certainly looks it," Andy said, magnetized by some power for which she had no name.

"What kind of gobbledegook are you two talking?" Lance wanted to know. "Can't you cut Tim and me in on this operation happiness?"

"I can see what they're looking at," Tim said. "But I don't see anything to get so steamed up about. A woman got pushed into the dining room in a wheel chair. Now she's sitting at a table."

"It looks as if she were paralyzed from the waist down," Andy said. "That's what I thought Martha meant. That I should be grateful I didn't get hurt in the river yesterday."

"Gratitude was not exactly what I had in mind," Martha said, rolling a scrap of toast between her thumb and forefinger.

"My curiosity is getting bigger than my appetite," Lance said. "Think I'll walk out to the desk and buy a paper so I can look over this marvel on the way back."

As he left the table Martha bent forward, speaking rapidly. "All your life, Andy, I think you've glorified courage—physical courage. That's one reason you love foldboating so much. Why you're so good at it—there's not a scrap of fear in you. Also, you're a competitor. You like to win. The river has been your antagonist and now because this once the river has beaten you, you're ready to fall apart. There are other kinds of courage, Andy. Harder kinds." Martha's voice was low but charged. "Courage to hope when there seems to be no hope, and——"

Tim was listening too now. "You mean like the people in Siberia, Mom? And the prison camps?"

"Yes, Tim. And there are people we never hear about,

like that girl over there in the wheel chair, who live
by sheer bravery of spirit. It's really very simple—it
isn't what happens to you that counts, but what you let
it do to you. That's a happy family over there—and you
know who makes it that way?"

Lance came back and handed the morning news to
his aunt. "It's an arresting face. I agree with you, Aunt
Martha. She looks as if she didn't have a care in the
world."

"Her skin is as smooth as her hair," Andy said, ad-
miring the long brown hair brushed straight back into
a knot as the Chinese women wear it.

"We've been talking about courage," Martha said, to
bring Lance back into the conversation again. "Body
courage and mind courage—but it's sort of early in the
morning for that kind of talk." The uncovered Martha
vanished. She became again the person Monk had described as "wonderful fun to have around."

"Want another bowl of oatmeal, Tim?"

"I'd rather have some eggs and bacon. Or maybe
just a couple of pieces of toast," he added quickly, sens-
ing some hesitation in his mother's face.

Lance asked, "How about my treating you to breakfast this morning, Tim? I meant to bring you a present
when I came down from Oregon. Then I didn't have
time to buy one. How would it be if instead of a present I staked you to all you can eat between here and
San Francisco?"

Tim looked doubtfully at his cousin. "Have you got
that much money? If I really let myself go I might eat
a good deal."

Equally serious, Lance pulled out his wallet and
counted the paper money. "I can feed you, Tim. But
if you overeat I won't be responsible for the hospital
bills."

Tim's "breakfast unlimited," as Martha called it, got

the day off to a cheerful start. Andy sent her mother
a wire saying, "Home for dinner tomorrow. Love,
Andy." Lance took the first trick behind the wheel and
in the back seat Andy retreated once more into her own
morass of regrets.

But with a difference. This morning the face of the
young mother in the wheel chair would not be erased
from her mind. Was it an accident? she kept wondering.
Polio? Was it temporary or permanent? She would
never know. Whichever it was, Andy knew that she had
seen a truly happy person. It's not what happens to you
that counts, but what you let it do to you. Martha was
probably right.

Also, during the long silences of desert driving, she
began to think about Buzz. For a week she had de-
spised him as a show-off and a bully. He boasted that
his football prowess made him "kind of a leader around
school." Am I like Buzz? Andy asked herself, going back
to Martha's other words about physical courage. Certainly Buzz had plenty of that. Am I a show-off too?
Interested only in how well I can paddle a boat? The
comparison did not sit comfortably in her mind.

After a time Tim interrupted this reverie. "Andy."

With a start Andrea pulled up out of herself. "Yes,
Tim."

"Andy. There's something I've been wanting to tell
you for quite a while. It's about me." Clearly Tim was
struggling.

"I'd like to hear it," Andy said softly.

Tim moved over closer. "Well—you know that morning you talked to me down on the beach about what
your father had said? It was just after we'd started.
Remember?"

Andy nodded wistfully, recalling that happy moment
in time.

"And I admitted I was scared of Lodore. Well—what

I wanted to tell you was that I've thought a lot about
the things you said that day. How being brave was
harder for some people than for others. And it helped,
Andy. Really it did."

"I'm glad of that, Timmie. It's funny you should
start talking about physical courage just now, because
it's exactly what I was thinking of."

"I just kept telling myself I didn't have to be as good
a foldboater as Lance, or you, or even Mom. That I'd
just be me. And me would be good at something else.
Then the funny thing was that right away I began to
paddle better. I guess Chuck noticed it too, or they
wouldn't have given me the prize that night at Jones
Hole. What were you thinking about courage, Andy?"

Andrea smiled wryly. "That the people who have it
are sometimes awful show-offs."

"You mean like Buzz?"

"I was thinking particularly of a girl I know who
cracked up in a foldboat."

"I guess it'll take the other kind of courage to break
that news to your family, won't it?"

"You're so right, Tim. It will take the kind that girl
in the wheel chair had—the kind that really matters."

"How about you and me having a private club,
Andy? We could call it the wheel-chair club and nobody would ever guess what we were talking about.
When we go foldboating we could tell each other about
any times we'd had wheel-chair kinds of courage."

The car had slowed for traffic in a little town and
abruptly Lance pulled in to the curb in front of a sign
reading, "Kim's Klassy Koffee Kup."

"Time to collect another installment on your present,
Tim," Lance said, opening the door for Martha and
Andy to get out.

When they had finished a leisurely hot drink they

changed drivers and Lance moved into the back seat
with Andy.

"What are you going to do when you finish school?"
he asked her after a long quiet spell.

"Go to college, I suppose," Andy answered. "I
haven't yet decided where. Wherever I can get in
probably. I'm no Phi Beta."

"I meant after college," Lance said. "College is school
too, in my language."

"Well—frankly I don't know—I haven't given it a lot
of thought."

"You haven't?" Lance pulled himself around in the
seat for a head-on look at Andy. "That's funny. In fact
it's *very* interesting."

"I fail to see why." Andy gave a rueful laugh.

"Because if you were a boy that just couldn't happen.
You might not have *decided* on a career, but you certainly would have sat through a lot of bull sessions on
the subject."

Andy kept silent. The last four years of her life she had
thought only of getting well and strong—and of foldboating.

"Do you think that's fundamental, Andy? A basic difference between men and women?" Lance took off his
dark glasses to wipe them on his handkerchief and Andy
could see clearly by his face that he was enjoying this
speculative kind of talk.

"I think it's because I'm lazy," Andy said.

"You're not, though."

"Well, get out your crystal ball. What do you see in
my future?"

"I've been wondering. That's why I asked. I can't
picture you spending eight hours a day indoors."

"Lady gardener, perhaps." It made Andy uncom-
fortable to have the spotlight turned on herself. "What

are you going to be, Lance?" she asked him. "Is it settled?"

"More or less. Architecture is the thing I'm shooting
for. Although the engineering angle may lick me. One
thing I'm really positive about. I won't be a salesman
of *anything*."

"I thought you might go in for professional photog-
raphy."

"Don't think I haven't chewed on that idea too. But
I believe a hobby is as much a part of living as doing
work you enjoy. I'd rather hold out my cameras for
that bird-chasing twerp." They both giggled reminis-
cently.

What to do after college seemed an incredibly distant
problem to Andy. Her real problem was what to do
when she got home—and what to say.

As Andy and Martha undressed that night in another motel in another town, she thanked Martha for
having made her change seats that morning at breakfast. "You gave me something to think about all day."

"You know, Andy, I've done some thinking too—
about you. I'm not sure it isn't a good thing for you to
have lost your first boat."

The shoe in Andrea's hand clattered to the floor. She
stared at Martha, not sure whether to be hurt or angry.

"But why? It's awful to lose a boat. Not just for me. It
hurts the whole sport. People read——"

Martha suppressed a smile. "I suppose it does. But
it may be that humility is one of the things you had to
learn, Andy. Life teaches us in peculiar ways sometimes."

"Oh, Martha, am I that stuck up? Am I like Buzz?
Tell me truthfully." She ran to Martha, kneeling on the
floor at her feet. "Am I just full of cocksureness and——"

"You're not a bit like Buzz. Except for one thing. Each

of you has the instinct of the born athlete—to win the game."

"And now I've lost." Andy spoke more to herself than to Martha. She got up from the floor, put her arms around Martha and kissed her. "You're a darling," she whispered.

"Because I've been lecturing you about feeling sorry for yourself? I'd feel sorrier for you if you had saved up for that boat penny by penny, baby sitting, or washing dishes for other people. Or if your family were church-mouse poor. But they're not, Andy. They can replace your boat without being hurt too much."

"I'll never ask for another."

"Then you'd better start advertising as a baby sitter the day after you get home." Martha had dropped another seed into the ground of Andrea's mind.

CHAPTER FIFTEEN

Ever since Lance had become the central figure in Andrea's secret world—that unspoken world which every girl carries about in her heart—she had thought of the day when she would introduce him to the family. She knew he planned to spend a little time in San Francisco before going back to Oregon. And on one of those days he would climb the steps to the house on Russian Hill and Andy would say, "Mother, this is Lance Ferrier. This is my father, my sister, Marianne. And Skeeter, my brother." The family would enjoy Lance as they used to enjoy Don.

Afterward Mother would say, "He has nice manners, Andy."

And Father, leaning his head against the back of the big chair, blowing pipe smoke toward the ceiling, would make his comment. "The boy's intelligent. His mind takes off into unexpected corners—not entirely surrounded by the collegiate fence."

Even Marianne, who had men waiting in line for dates, would approve. There was no forecasting what Skeeter would say. But at least he was old enough now not to make some embarrassing crack. He wouldn't burst out with, "Sure a long time since you brought a boy around, Andy." During dinner they would talk about the river trip and afterward Mother would bring coffee to the living room with the small white porcelain cups she always used for guests. They would sip coffee in front of a bright wood fire—there couldn't be a San Francisco evening too warm for a little fire after dinner —and as they looked into the flames she and Lance would remember the campfires they had watched together. Crackling driftwood, old logs crumbling into embers, stars overhead, and the soft misty smell of the river. Particularly they would remember their last campfire at Jones Hole. Across the room their eyes would meet while they sat there saying nothing, understanding everything.

Later in the evening Lance might take her to a movie, or perhaps drive up to Coit Tower where they could look out over the bridges crisscrossing the bay like necklaces of light and watch the whole jeweled city spread at their feet.

Well—it had been a lovely dream. Now she was a failure, a fool. Lance would not be interested in coming to dinner, nor would she embarrass him by asking. The first evening at home was a prospect that made her cringe.

But the reality turned out to be quite different from anything Andrea had dreaded or dreamed.

It was still daylight when Martha cramped her wheel against the steep curb in front of the Dawson house, turned off the motor, and handed the keys to Lance. As he opened the trunk of the car Andy plucked out her knapsack, slid a strap over one shoulder, and reached for her dunnage bag.

"Wait a minute, Andy. Not so fast. I'll carry those up for you. That's quite a flight of steps."

"Don't bother," she said. "I'm used to them."

Firmly Lance took the bag out of her hands. "Camping days are over," he said.

From the open trunk her two empty boat bags leered at her. Scooping them up, Andy held them against her chest as she leaned in at the open window of the automobile for a last word of thanks to Martha.

" 'By, sweetie," Martha said. "Tell your parents quickly about the boat and then forget it. See you in a week or two."

Andy started away, wheeled back to speak to Tim. "You're the president," she said solemnly.

"Okay. Then you're the vice," Tim called after her.

Feeling as if she were walking to the guillotine, she started up the familiar stairs ahead of Lance. As they neared the front porch the sound of piano music came rippling down to meet them.

"Hi-fi?" Lance asked, brightening visibly.

"No, it's my sister. She's practically that good, though." Again the old pang. Marianne gives people pleasure. All I give them is trouble.

Lance stopped to listen. "Sounds like Chopin."

"Which probably means my father is home. Dad's feeble about Chopin."

The front door was unlatched. Leaving it wide open, Andrea darted across the hall to the coat closet, hurled the boat bags into the farthest corner under the overcoats.

Upstairs Skeeter's sharp ears heard the front door open. Three steps at a time he came rocketing down. "Andy! Hello! Gosh, we thought you'd never get home. Mother's been in a tizzy since about four o'clock."

Lance still stood hesitantly in the open doorway. "Come on in," Skeeter said, closing the door behind him.

At that moment the rest of the family converged as if they had been hanging on the chandelier ready to drop when Andy arrived. Andy stood there looking at them, without moving, without saying anything at all. Their happiness was almost too much to bear.

"I'm Lance Ferrier," Lance said finally, holding out his hand to Mrs. Dawson. "Martha Frayne's nephew and one of the river trippers. I just carried Andy's bag up the steps for her," he added apologetically, turning to go.

"Oh, don't hurry away," Mrs. Dawson said.

Skeeter began looking around the hall. He opened the front door and looked on the porch outside. "Where's your boat, Andy? Those two big bag things. I'll carry 'em up the steps for you." He started out the front door.

"Tell them quickly," Martha had said, "and forget it." Forget she could not. But she'd get the telling over at once. Oh, why did Lance have to be here now to witness this second humiliation?

The stubby broken fingernails curled into her palms. "There isn't any more boat," she said doggedly. "I rode up on a rock. The boat broke in half. I . . ."

The big man with the gentle eyes moved across the circle and folded her into his arms, bending down until his lips touched her hair. "My little lemming," he murmured.

"What did you call Andy?" Skeeter demanded.

"Skip it, Skeeter." And Skeeter, who knew all the degrees of urgency in his father's voice, subsided instantly.

But Andy heard and understood. Chuck had talked about lemmings in class—those little mouselike creatures of Norway and Sweden which in certain years when food is scarce set out on mass migrations over fields and rivers, down, down, from the great central plateau until they drown themselves in the sea.

How Andrea had expected her family to react to her accident she had never really thought through. She knew, of course, they were not going to beat her. They might laugh, they might scold, they would surely say, "No more foldboating, young lady. It's too dangerous." The thing she was not prepared for was understanding. It surrounded her like a life preserver and buoyed her up. It was almost a tangible thing.

When she stepped back from her father's embrace Marianne caught her hand in a quick squeeze, stood there holding it while they talked to Lance.

Mother said, "What does a boat matter, darling, as long as you are safe?"

Even Skeeter stood quietly looking at her out of big sad eyes.

She was not suffering alone any longer, the whole family shared with her, and so the hurt became only one fifth as great as it was before.

Lance kept trying to get away, the Dawsons kept asking him questions. "Why don't you stay for dinner?" Mother said. "You'll probably tell us lots of things Andy will never think of mentioning."

"Not tonight, Mrs. Dawson. Thanks just the same. I'd like to help Martha unload the car. And I know she's anxious to get home because she starts back to work tomorrow."

It may have been that serene and radiant face which remained graven in Andy's mind, the face which said so clearly, "It's not what happens to you that matters, but what it does to you." Possibly it was because Lance had said, "Not tonight, Mrs. Dawson," meaning another night. Or perhaps when she came right to the point of realizing that she might never see him again, Andrea could not let him go.

"Will you have dinner with us some other night before you leave?" Andy asked, trying desperately to sound casual, the way Mother had sounded.

"Of course I will, Andy. I've been hoping you'd ask

me. I thought perhaps after your crack-up—it hit you
so hard—you never wanted to see any of your river
friends again."

"Of course I want to see them. They're the best
friends I have—except these." Her look took in the tight
little knot of family still standing in the hall.

"Tomorrow, Lance? Or the next day? I know you
aren't staying long."

"Tomorrow," Lance said.

"Half-past six," Mother called after him as he ran
down the steps to Tim and Martha waiting in the car.

Sharing a room once more with Marianne felt
strange. It was neither familiar, like sleeping on the
ground beside Finette and Martha, nor quite the same
as before she went away. Tonight Andy had drawn
closer to her own family than ever in her life. That
tense moment in the hall when Marianne impulsively
reached for her hand and stood clasping it tightly in
her own had broken a mold. Their lifelong pattern
of supervising older sister and stubbornly resisting
younger one had melted like snowflakes falling on warm
earth.

Usually the two girls undressed quickly, snapped off
their bed lights and went to sleep. But this evening
Andy needed to talk.

Marianne was bending over the basin with a toothbrush. Andy sat on the edge of her bed doing nothing
toward getting into it. At regular intervals a foghorn
out on the bay gave a melancholy blast.

Turning toward the open bathroom door, Andy
called, "Marianne?"

"Umm?"

"How much an hour do baby sitters get?"

"I've no idea. Why?" Between sentences Marianne
continued polishing her small even teeth with careful

up-and-down strokes. "Piano practice always kept me too busy to herd young. What's on your mind?"

"Nothing. I just wondered. Do you suppose the people in that big pink house on the next block need baby sitters? They have four children."

"Why this sudden interest in——? Oh! Now I get it." Marianne dropped her night toothbrush into the holder above the basin, walked over to sit down on the bed beside her sister. "You're thinking about another boat."

"Well——"

"Aren't you?"

"In a word—yes."

"I imagine Dad will get one for you—after Mother comes out of shock."

"I'd rather not ask. In fact I *won't* ask—not if it takes me years to earn the money."

"You've got spunk, Andy." Putting one slender hand under the stubborn sun-tanned chin, she turned Andy's face so that she could look straight into it. "Where do you find all that courage? If I'd taken a roughing-up like yours I'd never put my foot in another boat."

"That's because you're you, I guess," Andy said thoughtfully. "And I'm—well—I'm me. Besides, you've got boys for a hobby. And I think they take a harder kind of courage than foldboats do."

Marianne didn't laugh. She moved over to her dressing table and began on the nightly pin-curl routine. How pretty she is, Andy thought. Even in pin curls she's pretty.

"That's a nice boy you asked for dinner tomorrow night," Marianne said. "He likes you, Andy."

"He did."

"He does."

Andy shrugged away that notion, stood up and began peeling her clothes into a heap on the floor. "Oh, Lance likes everybody. He's just the friendly type."

When both their lights had clicked off Marianne
spoke from her own bed. "Tell me about this Lance,
Sis. Did you have fun together on the river trip?"

A sigh ran through Andy's whole body and her face
was turned half into the pillow as she whispered, "It
was won-der-full It's the first time, Marianne, the first
time since Don I've really had fun with a boy. Talked
to him without—without that scared feeling, sort of
wondering what to say next. Lance liked me, I think,
because I could handle a boat pretty well."

"Oh, Andy, no! Boys don't like girls because——"

"Well, why else would he? I'm not cute and feminine
like you. I don't have any big line or——" The pitch of
Andy's voice was soaring up the scale.

Marianne swung bare feet back to the floor again
and stood beside Andy's bed, stroking, ever so gently,
the top of her sister's head. "Andy darling. Don't say
things like that. Don't even think them."

There was no answer from the face buried in the
pillow. Sliding into bed beside her sister, Marianne
wrapped one arm around her shoulders. "Whatever
gave you the idea that you're not pretty?" she asked
tenderly.

"Years of experience," Andy mumbled.

"But you are. We're different types, that's all."

"I wish I'd learned to set my hair the way you do,"
Andy said, still into the pillow. "Maybe that would help
a little bit. My face is exactly the shape of a box."

"But I *love* your hair straight. It has body—and style.
Especially when you groom it. Fluttery hair like mine
wouldn't suit your face a bit."

Andy rolled over. "Do you really believe what you're
saying, Marianne, or are you just trying to make me
feel better?"

"I'm as sure of it as of anything I know. You've never

taken much trouble about clothes, Andy, or seemed to care how you looked——"

"Well, I care now! Though I don't know why. I'll never see Lance again after tomorrow."

"I wouldn't count on that. After all, he's only going to Oregon, not into Red China. But suppose your ways don't cross again—ever. It still isn't the end of the world. Believe me, pet, there are just as many good fish in the sea as ever came out of it."

"Fishing doesn't seem to be much in my line."

Marianne ignored this. "Every boy who comes into your life gives you something, Andy. Don did. And I'm sure Lance has too. He might have given you all the confidence in the world if you didn't have this silly idea that his liking you has something to do with the way you paddle a kayak."

"It isn't a kayak!" Andy sputtered. "It's a fold——" Then they both exploded into giggles. "This is where I came in," Marianne said.

They lay quietly for a time with their arms around each other, but Andy was far from sleep. "Do you think I should wear a dress tomorrow night or a sweater and skirt? I don't want to look all done up."

"I'd wear whatever makes you feel most comfortable, something you really like."

"That would be jeans."

"Oh *no!*" Andy could feel her sister curl with distaste.

"I admit my jeans are pretty sad-sack."

"Would you like me to help you decide? Have a look through your closet tomorrow? I'm not really sure what you own."

"Oh, would you, Marianne?"

"That's a date then. Right after breakfast."

"Right after I wash my hair," Andy corrected.

Andy was asleep when Marianne finally left her bed

for her own. "Poor baby," she murmured, looking at the tousled head lying in a shaft of light from the street lamp. "Poor mixed-up baby."

As if unconsciously she had been listening for it all night, the sound of her father's step on the stairs brought Andy wide awake the following morning. She looked at the clock. Dad must have an early appointment at the hospital. Hurrying to the closet for a bathrobe, she followed him into the kitchen.

He had his head inside the refrigerator, looking for a can of fruit juice, when Andy put her arms around him from behind. "It's that lemming again," she said.

"For heaven's sake, you? I thought you'd be sleeping till noon today."

"I heard you creeping down early. It's not seven yet. Here, let me make you some real coffee. I know you hate powdered." She took the jar out of his hands.

"No time for real coffee this morning. I've got a pretty sick man to see and early—may not be early enough. I'll eat later." He drank the juice, standing beside the teakettle, waiting for it to boil.

Shall I ask him now? Andy wondered. He's thinking about this patient with his whole mind. Better wait, I guess, till another time. He's just going into the rapids.

Her father sat down to gulp the scalding coffee and Andy sat opposite, a glass of tomato juice untouched on the table in front of her.

"I know what you want to ask me, Andy," her father said, coming out of his preoccupation for a moment. "Will I get you another boat? Isn't that it?"

"No, Dad. No. I don't want you to get me one." She leaned toward him fervently. "I only want to ask if I may buy one myself—when I finish earning the money for it."

She could see that the patient was pushed into the

background now. Surprise, disbelief, and finally a slow pride chased each other across her father's features.

"Have you a plan?" he asked slowly. "A hundred and seventy dollars is quite a bit of money to earn."

"Baby sitting is what I thought of. I suppose I'd have to start with kindergarten age. Nobody would trust me with an infant."

Still her father said nothing. Neither yes nor no.

"What I mean is—are you willing to *let* me go out with the River Runners again?"

"I certainly don't want my daughter to be a quitter," her father said huskily. He got up to leave, turned back in the doorway. "Tell you what I'll do, Andy. Every dollar you save toward the price of a new boat, I'll match with another dollar."

Andy ran after him, but he was already halfway to the garage.

After breakfast with the rest of the family Andy washed her hair, rinsed it with quantities of lemon juice, and brushed it dry until her arms ached. Then she and Marianne together explored her closet. There was not a great deal to choose from. Shorts, pedal pushers, slacks, and jeans in all stages of repair and disrepair, tee-shirts and boys' shirts. There were a couple of silk dresses—too done up, they both decided. School skirts, gray flannel or dark plaid, didn't seem quite right, and with the fog hanging over the bay as if it intended to spend the weekend, her one new cotton, the apple-green plaid Mother had bought just before she left home, looked definitely chilly.

"Where's that pink cashmere slip-on sweater the Boston aunts sent you last Christmas?" Marianne suddenly asked.

"In a box. I've never worn it because it has long sleeves and they get dirty in five minutes."

"Well, wear it now. That old rose-colored flannel skirt would look wonderful with it if you pressed it."

Andy pressed. She spotted and pressed again, until finally Marianne said, "It looks fine."

Fingernails were her worst problem. She worked at them a long time with a nailbrush, but the stains of camping appeared indelible. At half-past five Mother came to her rescue with a bottle of rosy nail polish which she applied with short precise strokes.

Andy sighed relief. "Oh, thank you, Mother."

"They do look better. Don't smear them now, will you? Give them time to get really dry." Mother kissed her as she got up to put the bottle away in its special niche in her dressing-table drawer.

"I'll stand just like this till dinnertime," Andy said, holding her arms out straight in front of her.

She wandered back to her own room and still with outstretched hands stood looking at herself in the long mirror. Still half an hour before Lance comes, she thought. He might be early, though. Marianne was in the kitchen. There was no one to talk to and she certainly couldn't concentrate on reading. So she continued standing in front of the mirror, looking hard, for perhaps the first time in her life, at the reflection which faced her. She liked what she saw.

"I'm Andrea Dawson," she whispered slowly to the pink sweater and the rose-colored skirt reflected in the glass. "I'm Andrea Dawson, who can never be a skier and who didn't turn out to be such a hot foldboater either. But she's going to try again. Because it's not your mistakes that matter—only what you let them do to you."

On a flash impulse Andy went to the old toy chest under the window and reached into the far right-hand corner. She could have found what she was looking for in the dark—the small box holding a pair of silver skis.

She opened the box, looked at the little pin, and laughed. Always before the sight of it had made her throat grow tight.

"It certainly is tiny," she said aloud, "and badly tarnished. But I don't need to hide it any more. What am I ashamed of? Don and I were best friends. We learned a lot from each other. Then we stopped being best friends. So what? Think I'll polish this up and wear it tonight!"

Andy flew down to the kitchen, fished the jar of silver cream from under the sink.

"Like my new medal, Marianne?" she asked impishly, fastening the small emblem over her heart.

"It's a nice touch," Marianne said. "Where've you been keeping it all these years?"

The face above the pink sweater smiled confidently. "In moth balls. But I've just discovered that's the wrong treatment for silver."

The doorbell rang and Andy fled to open it.